D1274785

The End of Summer

John Lowry Lamb

SIMON & SCHUSTER

New York London Toronto

Sydney Tokyo Singapore

SIMON & SCHUSTER
Rockefeller Center
1230 Avenue of the Americas
New York, NY 10020

This book is a work of fiction. Names, characters, places, and incidents either are products of the author's imagination or are used fictitiously. Any resemblance to actual events or locales or persons, living or dead, is entirely coincidental.

Designed by Deirdre C. Amthor

Manufactured in the United States of America

1 3 5 7 9 10 8 6 4 2

Library of Congress Cataloging-in-Publication Data
Lamb, John Lowry.
The end of summer / by John Lowry Lamb.
p. cm.
I. Title.
PS3562.A4233E5 1995
813′.54—dc20 94-46865
CIP
ISBN 0-684-80358-5

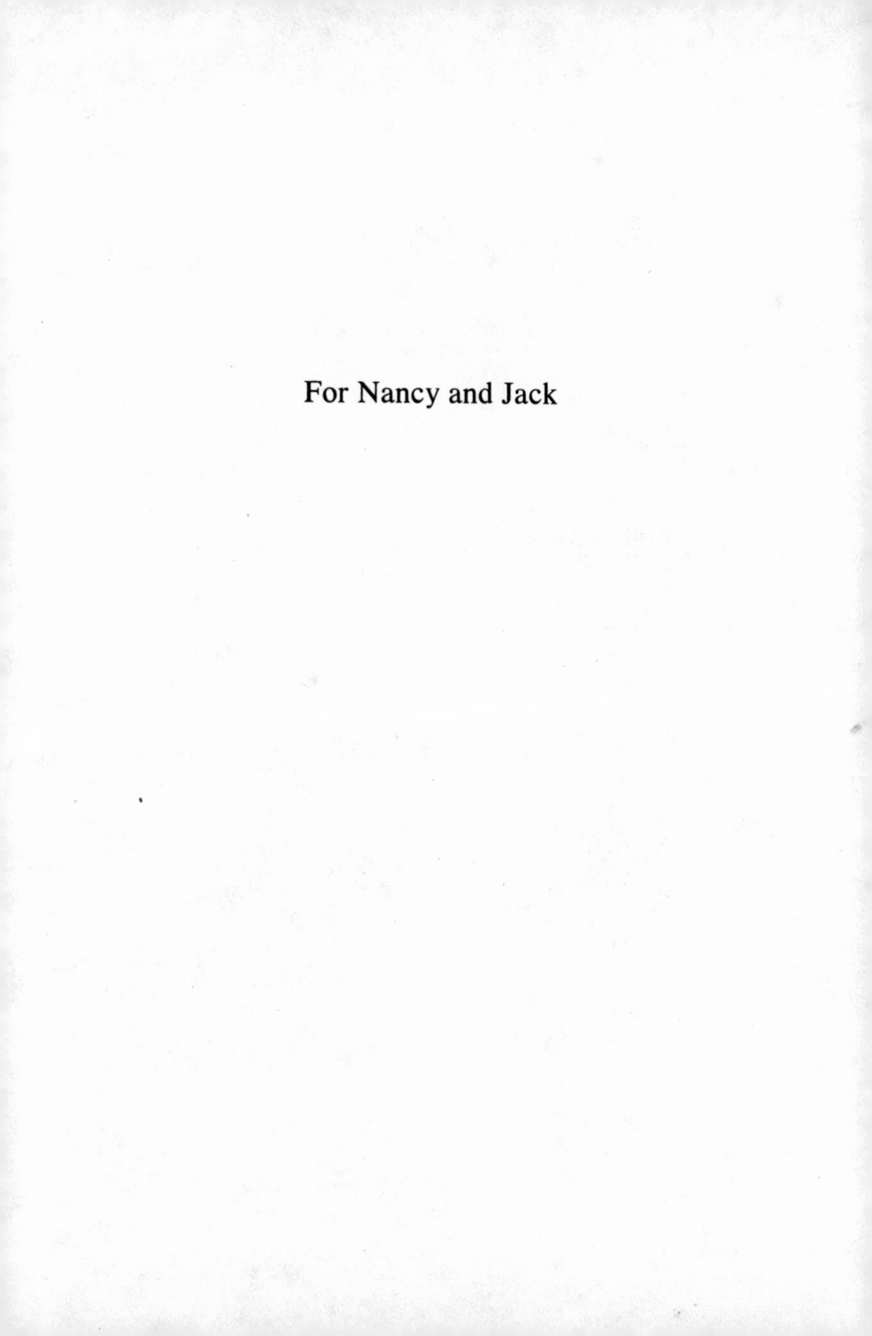

For Nancy and Jack

Acknowledgments

Charles F. Adams, editor and guide;
Michael Korda, bringer to light;
Michael Sheresky, Matthew Bialer and
Amy Schiffman, sharers of a rare sight
and
Chelsea Pinehurst, Lord of Van Ness.

Spirits of the Erie

BRAVES' Point. A flat-topped hill in upper Ohio, carved away ages ago by melting glaciers.

A high hill, by Ohio standards, but not so steep that it couldn't be climbed. It rose steadily, gradually, a quarter mile, and from the top one could see the dips and curves of the landscape below, its lumpy earth and slight valleys creeping around Sharon Lake, until the horizon rose up and said, "No more."

At the bottom of the hill stood an old man and a young boy, looking upward, still, as if frozen in their tracks, eyes focused on something.

The boy glanced quickly at his companion and then up again at the two deer, a buck and doe, legs speared into the hillside. Godly, magical.

"Look at 'em, Doc," the boy said, his voice full of awe.

He watched the old man, Dr. James F. Dugan, raise his

finger to his pursed lips; the boy did the same. Together they smiled, sharers of a rare sight.

"I'll be damned," said the Doc, his voice a whisper.

"Uhh . . ." the boy gasped. The sound came out as just a breath. He'd never before been so close to wild animals like these. So large. He shut his eyes, feeling his blood surge through his veins. Pounding in his ears. Why? He'd seen a lot of animals, had raised and cared for many of them. But these were different—strong, alien, absolutely at peace. What is it about them? he wondered.

He opened his eyes again. The buck and doe were as before, still frozen in place—but now they were looking him square in the eye, staring him down.

Something wasn't right, though.

For a moment, for just a few seconds, the real world seemed to lose its hold. Sure, the deer were there, and he was there, *and the Doc . . .*

But things weren't in order. Not the way they were supposed to be. The antlers on the buck's head looked—fake, he thought, stuck on . . .

And the Doc . . . He turned to look at the old man. There he is, his still face almost transparent, like thick plastic. Not real. Nothing is real.

No.

• • •

Of course it is all real. The boy shook his head. What am I thinking?

Adrenaline. Sloshing around in his brain. His mind buzzing. He felt good yet horrified at the same time. He, and the Doc, and the deer, caught up in a few time-warped moments. Then bang, the spell was broken. The buck lurched first, then the doe, and together they ran, taking the hill. And when they did, the boy thought it was a wonderful sight.

He caught his breath, then exhaled, smiling as he did. "Wow, ohhh." He looked at Doc Dugan, who stared in silence. A teardrop fell from the old man's eye.

"Nickie?" the Doc said. "Thirty-pointer. I'll be damned . . . thirty-pointer . . . ," and the boy watched the two glorious animals bolt up the hillside as if on stilts that barely touched the ground.

Within minutes, Nick Harper was trudging up the slope alone, following the narrow, winding footpath of Braves' Point Hill, carrying with him every second of his dozen years. What does my life mean? he wondered silently. And then aloud, to the wind: "What does my life mean?"

He stopped, ready for an answer. Hoping for an answer. But there wasn't one. Not on *that* day.

• • •

At the very top, Braves' Point Hill leveled, forming a natural plateau about a hundred yards square. Centuries of nature's handiwork had made a friendly meadow there—a field, confined in empty space, held in place by grass-covered cliffs. And in that field at the very top, in the very center, lay two Indian burial mounds.

The boy passed the snake-shaped graves, bowing his head as he always did in reverence to the old dead bones buried below.

"Good morning," the boy said aloud.

"Hello, Nick," a voice replied.

• • •

Six months had passed since the cold and unfriendly January morning when his life was turned upside down, when his joy and innocence were lost, frozen by the winds of winter. But now, on this warm June day, he sat in the Braves' Point meadow, looking at the ancient graves, the two strange lumps of earth, struggling to get a grasp on his sorrow, deep in conversation with his phantoms.

A Year Ago

THE day was mostly gone as Nick made his way home along the riverbank. He came to a place he knew well, where he and his father had spent many nights and early mornings going after bass and catfish. They called it the fishing hole. Underneath the water the river bottom dropped severely. There in the deep, cool water the big fish sought refuge from the summer sun.

Now it all seemed so long ago, so out of his grasp. His eyes scanned the site, an area of ground worn down to the dirt, the river beyond it and the opposite shore, the logs stacked up, the tree stumps, the half-bare branches of the trees, thick, climbing forty feet above him.

Some Styrofoam containers and soda cans still lay about; small balls of fishing line, remnants of snags of the past tangled in the bushes, quivered in the slight breeze. All the elements combined made the place seen alive.

Then he saw something shiny . . . something familiar.

He went toward it; it was exactly what he thought, a fishing lure, with yellow-and-black feathers and a metal stem, a spinner and turning spoon. It seemed impossible but there it was, his father's favorite lure, the one he said could never fail, yet never worked.

Was it possible? Had it been there an entire year, and no other fisherman had found it?

He picked it up, feeling it, reading its history. The paint had held up well, but the hook was rusted. Rust, he thought. Perfect. Amazing how the sight of so little an object could cause so much pain.

He trembled and his eyes filled with tears as he fought to control himself. His knees weakened, and he lowered himself into a squat. My father, he thought, *my* dad, the man his mother called Charles . . . where are you?

He didn't want to cry again. Not now. He had to get angry. That always helped to stop the tears.

He sat on the ground and breathed, pulling in oxygen, battling the anxiety. His psychologist had told him to do it—don't resist the anxiety; meet it, head on, and *breathe* . . .

Ten deep breaths. Relax. There, that's better.

"It's not fair," he said aloud, his voice clear and steady. "It's just not fair."

In a few minutes he felt better. Still holding the lure, he stared at it, rubbed it, looking for more pleasant vibrations of that summer night, a year ago.

Gradually he lay back and looked at the clouds, listened to the river. The slow gush of the water calmed him, even made him tired, and he let himself remember . . . a night . . . with his father. Cat fishing. In the darkness. The Coleman lamp, throwing just enough light . . .

• • •

That whole day Nick had wanted to go fishing, but Charles was in his study with the door closed and Nick could hear the adding machine clicking away. He knew that meant his father was "doing the money," and that meant stay out of his way. Nick waited through a long stretch of silence and then went in. Charles was writing checks. Nick worked on him for an hour, beginning with "How ya' doin', Pop?" and ending with "Do you know it's eighty-seven degrees outside tonight? The cats'll be hitting like mad!" And finally Charles gave in. "For an hour," he said, "one hour, Nick. Okay?"

"Yes."

"See my hand? How many fingers?"

"One."

"Right. One. *One* hour."

Nick knew better. Knew that once Charles got into something, there was no time.

They arrived at the fishing hole and set up their rods. For the first hour they didn't get a nibble. Charles, who had been drinking beer, moved slightly into the woods to relieve himself. Nick waited a moment, then knocked the fishing pole with his hand, and yelled, "You got a hit! Dad!" Charles came running back, zipping up as he did. He crouched, watching his fishing rod settle. "It was big, Dad. He really hit it."

"Catfish, man . . . ," Charles said, sitting back intently, and Nick knew he had him for the night.

The moon seemed especially proud—it was so bright that it washed out the stars and it smoothly lit the two figures crouching there by the river. The whizzing bugs and the sound of crickets and the moving river hypnotized them, got them in the mood. They stayed until three o'clock in the morning, huddled around the glowing mantles of the lamp.

On that night they snagged six catfish and a carp who was up well past his bedtime. At one point Charles was talking and not watching his line. Nick saw it bobbing. Charles pulled the line, which set the hook, and he reeled in. "Small one . . . ," he said, and it was. A baby catfish. It had swallowed the hook whole.

Charles explained the sad situation. The hook had gotten caught in the stomach of the fish. If they cut the line and put him back in the water, the fish would surely die. But there was no way to get in and take the hook out; the aperture of his mouth was too small. The most merciful thing to do, he said, would be to kill it.

Nick didn't like any of the choices, but deferred to his father's judgment. Charles stood, and with all his might, slammed the fish down onto the surface of the water. The fish was instantly dead. Nick watched it floating, lifeless.

Charles used the opportunity, in his easy way, to begin a discussion about death. Nick figured later he must have been watching out for the right moment—death, and dying, had been on his father's middle-aged mind a lot. Nick didn't look at his dad as being old. Still he *was* forty-four, his time on earth half over in the span of a normal life.

Charles started by talking about trees—how they had a life, and a death. Then he talked about the fish, then everything else. Life, death. Then he said, "You, too, Nick. You'll die, too."

"Wow," Nick had answered, aware that his response was inadequate. Then he was quiet for a while.

Finally Nick reeled in his line, set his fishing pole aside, and turned to his father with questions, and never stopped for an hour straight.

"So what about heaven? Is there one or not? . . . Wow, I'll be dead. My body dead, wow, and you, too. Dad . . . how do you feel about being dead someday? Does it bother you? . . . and how do they know you're dead? What if you wake up in your coffin? Why do we have to die? When the body dies, what about the part of us that thinks? Do we continue to think?"

Charles answered him clearly and directly, taking plenty of time before giving each answer, never hesitating to say honestly that he wasn't sure about something if he wasn't. Finally Nick asked, "You won't die—for a long time, right?"

Exactly five heartbeats later, Charles said, "I don't know."

Normally Nick was pleased to hear the response "I don't know"; he felt a sense of accomplishment when someone *didn't know* an answer to one of his questions. But as he watched his father struggling to answer him, he grew frightened. He knew his father to be a man who always had something to say on any subject. So why now the sudden blank?

Suddenly Nick was aware that his father wanted to get off the subject, and trying to mask his own sense of relief, he played along. But an hour later, he said to Charles, "By the way, Dad, thanks. You—think about—what *I'm* thinking . . . ," tapping his temple as he said it.

"What you're thinking. Yes . . ."

• • •

And now, sitting at the fishing hole in the mid-June sun thinking back on that night, Nick wondered if Charles finally knew all the answers, wherever he was.

Dusk. Justine might be a little angry, he realized, since he had probably missed dinner. Of course it would depend on what stage of her nightly routine she had reached. The wine brought her up for a while, but then she would get irritable for an hour before she went to bed. The drinking usually began around six, while she was cooking. But often, especially when Nick was not there during the day to *see* her start drinking, she would begin as early as four o'clock, and was cranky by dinner.

Nick looked at his Space Shuttle watch. It was 7:30; that was very late. He *knew* his aunt would be angry. Still he was anxious to get home. He would have to hurry if he wanted to see his mother before she fell asleep.

The Golden Comet

NICK crossed the corn and soybean fields. They lay dead, still, at a time of year when normally they would be battlefields of activity. This year they were nothing. There had been no seed, no care, and the empty soil lay baking under the day's last rays of sun.

Approaching from the back way, he neared the barn, and just beyond it, the remains of the shed—which he had burned down at Christmas, seven months ago. He looked at its black-charcoaled beams and studs, half standing, holding up nothing.

The fields ran on either side of the house, parallel stretches running up to the road on one side and back to the edges of the woods on the other. And what once had been meticulously cared for rows of earth were now black and bare, the only sign of life the encroaching summer weeds. Symbols of better times were everywhere—the John Deere tractor that Charles had been so proud of finally being able to afford; the newly painted house; the backboard and basketball hoop screwed into the elm tree; the curtains his mother had made; even the rooster, scowling in his pen, no longer studding and not too happy about it—all reminders of what had been and what was lost.

As he walked, he thought about that rooster, and about the day he and his father had bought him.

Nick had gone with Dad on a Saturday morning, one of many; it was their time together, away from the farm, traveling on strange country roads and in little towns. On that day, they drove in a borrowed truck to nearby Alliance, ending up at a very unusual person's house—a fat man, with scrawny children, in a run-down, falling-down house with a filthy kitchen. It was an odd storehouse of goods—boxes of canned foods, agricultural chemicals, and turkeys and chickens penned up in separate crates with a smell so strong that it was hard to stay in there too long. Nick kept going outside for air while his father looked over the merchandise. He examined the hens, asking the man to remove them one at a time from the crates so he could inspect the fluff of their tails and the redness of their combs. Some were sickly but he found five Rhode Island Reds in good-enough shape—he could bring them up to snuff with regular feedings and some liberation.

Nick appeared in the doorway holding a hen. "Dad, can we take this one home?"

Charles could tell from the pale wattle under its chin that it was not a good specimen. "We've got five good ones here, Nick."

"It's a Golden Comet," Nick said.

"Well, all right," his father had said, nodding first to his son, then to the man. "We'll take the five Reds and the Golden Comet."

The ride back to Sharon Lake was so terrible it became hilarious. The car smelled so bad they had to roll the windows down and drive with their heads out the windows. After a while they began laughing, holding their noses and gasping for fresh air.

That day, those days, were gone.

• • •

Nick slowed as he passed the barn. His eyes rested for an instant on the family's blue pickup truck, then the coop. Inside the chickens clucked in pulses; they sounded comfortable, snuggled into their hay bales. The rooster complained, however, separated from his harem, enclosed in a small area adjacent to the coop. Justine had mentioned the day before that she intended to sell the rooster soon. The family was no longer in the business of breeding chickens, she had said, so from now on they would keep only six hens—enough to provide a supply of eggs.

As he approached the house, Nick stood for a moment, looking at it. Though it was old—built in the 1920s, his father had told him—one could hardly tell. Just a year ago, Charles had restored it, and like everything he had ever touched, it was immaculate. He had caulked every crack, scraped it, sanded it, painted it. Nick, of course, had helped, too, holding ladders and cleaning out brushes. And every day his mother had made lunch; the three of them would sit on the lawn and eat. Nick remembered being proud that he was marked with paint just like his father. It made him feel—adult. Nick wasn't sure what he felt now. That summer, the last summer, had been a wonderful time. It had been just the three of them, together, happy.

Things were so different now. In such a short time.

• • •

He stepped onto the wood-slat porch. It had been a popular place for his parents; there, Charles and Mary Lee and their guests sat most nights when the weather was fair, sometimes smoking marijuana and talking, and drinking and laughing. And listening to the Rolling Stones. Two audio speakers, ruined now, their mesh covers loose, their wires dangling, were still hung there, forgotten.

Nick had enjoyed his parents' friends, and even the occasional strangers who had come to visit. Nice, intelligent, down-to-earth sort of folks, who came from local universities for field studies. Nick found the professors and students easy to entertain, and he talked with them, watching their manners, learning their speech. Nick assumed the responsibility for giving all newcomers a tour of the farm, commandeering the tractor and hay wagon. And all visitors in turn seemed enchanted with this precocious boy, and with the farm and its easy lifestyle, and especially with Charles and Mary Lee whose graciousness was endless. Their inner contentment, born out of a twenty-year mad crush on each other, rubbed off on all that came into their company.

All that was over. Now Nick stood alone on the porch, remembering those good times. Six months had passed since the fatal day, and while he was out of shock, he was still in deep mourning, still unable to accept the emptiness that threatened never to go away.

Finally he entered the house and greeted Justine, who sat at the kitchen table with a glass of red wine in front of her.

"Where've you been, Nickie?" she said, her words slurring slightly.

Nick knew what that meant; the next morning she would not remember anything that had been said, which he figured was just as well. "Mmm . . . out," he answered as he crossed to the refrigerator.

"Did you get the mail?" she asked.

"Yes, it's on the porch."

He fished out a carton of orange juice and drank from the container.

"Nickie, please use a glass," Justine said.

"It's almost gone. I'm gonna finish it, okay?"

Justine sipped her wine. "Well, are you going to get it?"

"Get what?"

"The mail," she said.

Nick looked at the floor. He wanted to say something, but hesitated. "Yes. I'll get it," he said. Then, unable to resist, "But I don't see—why—" He stopped.

"Why what?" she said.

"Why *you* can't get it."

He expected her to be angry. Instead, she peered silently into her glass.

Angry now, Nick continued. "I mean don't your feet work? Are your legs broken or something?"

Nick drained the juice and tossed the empty carton into the trash can. Justine was silent still. He sensed that he had touched on something, something she didn't care to discuss. "I'm gonna go see Mom," he said, and left the room.

Justine rapped her fingernails on the table rapidly. Twice.

. . .

Nick quietly cracked open the door to his mother's room. He saw her awake in bed, covered up almost to her chin by her favorite quilt, her eyes blank and distant, staring straight ahead—as they always did. It frightened Nick, the way his mother lay, motionless, her frail arms crossed on the blankets over her chest. "Mom?" he said, softly. She didn't answer. He moved quickly to her side. "Mom?"

Her head rolled to the side. "Nickie-bird . . ."

He reached up and touched her hand. He covered it with his own hands, noticing how warm his were in comparison; she's cold, he thought, she has no life.

She said to him, "How you doin'?"

"I'm all right . . . I was here. This morning. Do you remember?" he asked.

"Yes," she answered, though not convincingly, "I remember."

"Do you need another blanket?"

"No, Nickie. I'm fine. I need to sleep. I'm tired."

Nick said nothing for a full minute. He lowered his forehead onto his knuckles. He thought for a long time, and before he left, he said, "I love you, Mom." She was asleep.

. . .

He went to his bedroom and put on his pajamas. But it was early, and he sat on the edge of the bed, wondering how he would occupy the rest of his evening. A few magazines lay on his bedside table, but they didn't interest him. He had recently been playing with his chemistry kit, trying some of the experiments described in the manual, but he wasn't in the mood for that either. What he really wanted was companionship. Deciding finally that Justine probably had enough energy left in her for a game of cards, he went downstairs.

She was in the living room, seated in the center of the couch, a half-full wineglass in her hand, watching television. Nick stood in the doorway behind her, watching. She laughed at something on the TV, not aware of Nick.

Who was Justine? Nick wondered as he looked at her. Sure, she was his father's sister, but why was she so different? She and Charles were opposites, really—he'd had such vitality; she could put one to sleep with her long looks and sad puffy eyes. He stood, reconsidering his plan. A card game would prove to be a long, silent activity, with Justine growing more drunk as time passed.

No, the notion of the card game no longer appealed to him. He turned quietly and walked down the short hallway leading to his father's study. Reluctantly, he pushed the door with his foot. This was a room he had avoided. The last time he had gone in there, months back, books were still open as Charles had left them, and the desk was covered with a mess of notes and papers. Nick had found it hard to be there, and had not stayed. Now the room was tidy.

Yet just being there was still painful, and he had to fight back the urge to turn and run. When he finally went in the room, he stood with his hands in his pockets for a full minute, just looking. Then he sat in the swivel chair at the desk. After a while he opened a few of the drawers and pushed the contents around. He pulled out a white folder crammed with loose papers, and began sifting through what seemed to be an unrelated accumulation of excerpts, handwritten by Charles, transposed from various sources: Plutarch, Samuel Johnson, Shakespeare and others. He picked a few out at random and read them, stopping at one passage written out with particular care in fountain pen. It was short, and was centered on a sheet of paper all by itself. Nick stared at it, reading it over several times.

It said, "Between grief and nothing, I will take grief," and the author's name, William Faulkner, was noted underneath it.

What does that mean? Nick thought. Nothing? No feeling? Can grief be better than that somehow? he wondered. I don't get it. How could anything be worse than what I feel, how sad I feel? Even when I forget, it doesn't last.

Grief over nothing? Better nothing over grief.

Justine appeared in the doorway. "I'm going to bed, Nickie."

"Oh, all right," he said, swiveling his father's chair.

"You all right?" Justine asked, her words slurred, running together.

"I'm fine," he said, remaining in the chair staring at her.

The moment turned awkward. He knew she wanted him to kiss her good night, and while he didn't want to hurt her, he just didn't *feel* it . . .

"Nick . . . where were you all day today?" she asked finally, breaking the long silence.

"We talked about this, remember?" he said.

"Come on, Nickie," she said, stumbling into the room. She stood next to him, holding on to his chair. "Tell me what you did today."

"Well, I just—went walking, really. Went to Braves' Point. Had a walk with Doc Dugan. Sat by the river. Then came home," he said, matter-of-factly.

Justine leaned down and hugged his head and kissed his hair. He felt embarrassed yet at the same time couldn't deny that it felt good. He was surprised that the rare moment of affection was even happening. It wasn't like her.

Their eyes met and they smiled at each other. Justine stroked his head and then walked out of the room, trying, but failing, to do it gracefully.

Nick listened as Justine clumped up the stairs. He stayed where he was, in his father's chair, thinking for a long time. Eventually he fell asleep. Finally he found peace.

• • •

In the morning, there were a number of chores to be done before he was free for the day. The chickens had to be fed, the eggs gathered and taken inside. The cows needed milking, something he hated, but knew he had to do, because it was dangerous *not* to milk them. So he lumbered out to the barn and slid the door back. As if attacking, the hens charged at him.

"Hey, you goofs," he said, brushing them aside with his foot. He dipped into a bag of feed and threw several handfuls onto the grass outside the barn. He watched as they ran after the food, waddling their way out into the early morning sun.

As he turned back to the barn, he realized that one chicken had stayed inside. It knew the routine, that Nick would next pour the grain for the cows, and that some always fell onto the ground, free for the taking. The chicken probably found it a better breakfast than the usual feed, and besides, it could eat without the bother of the other chickens now scrambling out in the yard.

That's the *smart* chicken, Nick thought. That's the Golden Comet.

Now the ordeal of the cows. He enticed them into a stall by waving some hay at them. As they ran in, he closed the stall door, trapping them inside. After a little chasing, he got lead ropes on them, then took them out of the stall one at a time and tied them to a hitching post. He poured grain into a feeder, set up the milking stool, and while they ate, he milked them.

That chunk of his morning chores done, he took a break and sat on a bale of hay, watching the cows as they ate. Very peaceful, he thought, the munching of cows. Then as he let them out into the corral, he noticed something white shoot out of the barn. It ran much too fast to be a chicken, and was way too big to be a rat.

Nick raced around the corner, scattering chickens in all directions. He stopped, his eyes searching.

Then he saw it again. Behind the bushes on the fence. He slowly walked toward it.

It was a white cat, already full grown, not hiding, just sitting there, staring at him with a calm superiority, as if to say, "I'm here. I'm staying here. Get used to it."

As Nick moved toward the cat, it sprang from the fence and disappeared into the brush. Nick stood still, listening, looking for moving weeds. But then he heard a loud noise, raucous enough to chase away anything.

Nick turned as a Jeep with a blown muffler pulled into the long driveway. A Wagoneer. Who could it be? he wondered. Very few people came to the farm anymore.

Justine came out onto the porch and pointed to the rooster pen, then walked down to meet the driver.

Nick had seen the man before but didn't know his name. The man had been one of the people at his father's funeral. Seeing him brought back a terrible memory, familiar and disturbing. Once again Nick saw himself standing by the hole in the ground, that awful yet intriguing hole.

Nick wandered over to Justine and the man. They were bargaining over a price for the rooster. She wanted ten bucks for the bird, he was offering five. They settled at seven.

Nick stared at the man's face, remembering him. That face looking at the casket as it was being lowered into the hole. Why couldn't it have been him, Nick had thought at the time. His face was old, his life was played out. Why is my father dead, and this man still alive . . . ?

Nick knew that if it were his father buying a rooster, and someone asked ten bucks, he would've paid, no questions asked.

It was so unfair. That's what hurt. That's what Nick could not understand. Why was an old, shifty man like this one allowed to live, while a good, vital person like his father had to die?

Nick didn't like those thoughts, didn't like these memories. He wished the man would just go away. He wished Justine would go away. He wanted to be left alone with his mother, left alone as a family to ride out this tragedy.

The man soon wrangled the bird into a steel cage and

drove off. As the Wagoneer pulled away, Justine waved at Nick. He rolled his fingers out in reply. When Justine was gone, he walked to the rooster pen and stared at the emptiness.

Just then the white cat darted out from behind the coop.

"Hey," Nick yelled out, and ran after it, following it into the barn.

Once again it was gone. Just disappeared. Nick searched for a half hour, and finally gave up. It just wasn't there. It seemed impossible.

It must have vanishing powers . . . , he thought.

As he left the barn, his ears caught another sound—the mail truck. He looked at his watch; it was ten after two—very late for the postman to come by. Mr. Digny never came later than eleven.

Nick ran down the driveway to meet the white Jeep. "Mornin'—I mean good *afternoon,* Mr. Digny," he said as he approached.

"Fine, just fine," was the answer, Arthur Digny's meet-all response.

"Late today, huh," Nick said as he took the mail.

"Little sick this mornin', Nickie. Late start."

"Well I hope you're feeling better," Nick said.

"Can't really talk today, gettin' chased by the clock."

"Oh, well . . ."

Digny cranked the truck into gear. " 'Bye, now . . . ," he said as he drove off.

• • •

Three *National Geographic* magazines were in the stack of mail. Nick was glad to see two back issues; he had been waiting for them. He tucked the whole pile under his arm, walked to the house, and dropped it on the porch. Before he left for the afternoon, he scanned the compound once again, looking for that white cat. But of course it wasn't there.

The News

NICK was up early the next morning. He had walked the long driveway to get the newspaper, and was sitting at the kitchen table drinking coffee and reading, long before Justine was awake. He quickly skimmed through the newly arrived magazines, his attention drawn to one issue in which most of the articles dealt with the destruction of the environment. He hardly looked up when Justine entered, looking disheveled and slightly hung over. She poured some coffee and sat at the table with her elbows resting on the paper that Nick had put there for her.

"Thursday's Dr. Kemper, Nick."

Nick shifted his eyeballs. "Yeah . . . I know," he said with a tinge of disgust.

Justine always read the weather report first. "Storm heading our way," she said, "summer storm."

"We need one," Nick said. "It's too dry."

This was typical morning talk. Nothing significant, mostly surface. Few questions, short statements.

"Oh, my God!" Justine said suddenly, her hand going to her mouth.

Nick looked up, instantly concerned. "What's the matter?"

Justine, her eyes now wide open, stared at the front page. "Oh, my God," she repeated.

"What? What is it?" Nick said, alarmed now.

She held up her finger as she finished the article. Then, instead of explaining, she handed the newspaper and went into the living room. Nick could hear her crying.

His eyes immediately went to the headline: TRAIN KILLS TWO. For a moment he closed his eyes; he didn't want to read it, didn't want to know who it was. He set the paper aside and tried to concentrate on his *National Geographic,* but in a few minutes he could hear Justine speaking on the phone. He leaned back in his chair so that he could see her. He watched as she gestured, ashes falling from her cigarette.

Did she know the people? he wondered. He knew she had grown up in Sharon Lake, but she hadn't lived there in a long time. Must've been a very old friend.

He sat for a while, half-listening through the doorway. Finally he picked up the paper again. He stared down at a photograph of a family, dressed in their Sunday best, posed in front of their fireplace, all smiling. The caption identified the two fatalities, a mother and daughter. A nine-year-old son had miraculously survived the accident.

Nick knew the girl from school, but instead of sadness he felt a kind of empty anger. He knew that in a home not far away, the relatives of the dead were just waking to a sad and different life.

Justine had known the mother years back, had gone through school with her, and while she hadn't seen her in fifteen years, the news seemed to hit her hard. Nick heard some of her comments: relief that death had come quickly, gratitude that the boy was only slightly injured. And over and over, she repeated, "What a terrible thing . . ." After she said it one too many times, Nick knew he had to escape.

He closed his eyes, and with all his willpower emptied from his mind the tragic news. He didn't want it in there. But all the wishing in the world could not erase the anger he felt, anger for God, or whoever it was responsible for this tragedy, for all the tragedies.

He went into the living room and signaled to Justine.

"Just a minute," she said into the phone. She covered the mouthpiece. "Yes, Nick?"

"You okay?" he asked gently.

"Yes, I'm fine," she said.

"I'm goin' out," he said, and she nodded.

• • •

He walked down his driveway to Stanepote Road, turned left, and made the one-mile trek to Doc Dugan's house.

He found the Doc in his usual spot, next to the front-yard pond, seated, as he always was, in his aluminum folding chair. Nick thought he looked sad, like death was hanging around his shoulders.

It was Charles who had first insisted on inviting the Doc to family dinners. Nick was only three years old at the time, and the Doc made him uncomfortable. Over time, though, they became the best of friends, and eventually Nick became the one who invited the lonely old man over, sometimes as often as three times a week.

Now, of course, there were no more family dinners, so the Doc rarely left his house. He and Justine didn't know each other, and she was more or less a hermit in her own way. Now, Nick and Doc's relationship was confined to these afternoon visits that Nick had come to look forward to, even to *need.*

"Catch old Granddad yet, Doc?" Nick asked as he sauntered up to the pond.

"He's too old, too smart. Only thing in the county older than me, that bass."

Nick slid off his shoes and sat, running his toes through the cool grass.

"How's your mom?" the Doc asked.

"Mmm, same," Nick said, and lay back on the grass. "Achy. Tired."

"Well, Nick, she needs you. You can help her by being with her."

"I do, Doc. Believe me."

"You're a good boy, Nickie." The Doc stopped abruptly. His fishing pole was quivering, ever so slightly. "See that? See it move?" he said, very quietly.

Nick nodded, careful to be quiet, knowing that only noise could scare the fish away.

The Doc whispered. "Smellin' it."

Nick smiled. He nodded, a sign of optimism, then said softly, "Granddad."

After another few seconds, the line settled again. The fish hadn't taken the bait.

Nick stood up. "Well, Doc, I'll leave you to it. I really

just came by to say hi. I . . . uh, had to get away . . . to get out. I better get goin'," he said.

"Where to?"

"Braves' Point. Just gonna hang out."

The Doc nodded. "Used to go there myself. When I was a boy." He turned and looked Nick square in the eye. "Ever . . . heard anything up there?"

Nick was stunned. He knew immediately what Doc was talking about, but he played dumb. "Like what?" he asked.

"Voices?"

This is strange, Nick thought. "Sure . . . plenty of times," he answered cautiously. "You, too?"

The Doc nodded, slowly, deliberately. A chill ran down Nick's spine. Doc's words verified something that had been unresolved in his mind—the reality of the voices. Though it frightened him that someone else had heard them, he also felt relieved. And vindicated—everyone had told him he was imagining things. Well, he was right after all. *Someone else* had heard the voices, too. He couldn't wait to tell that to his psychologist, Dr. Kemper. It had been a source of conflict between them all summer.

"Well, I'll catch ya later, Doc," Nick said, starting toward the woods.

"Bye Nick," the Doc said, giving the boy a wave.

What a contrast between Doc Dugan and Dr. Kemper, Nick thought as he walked along. There was something heartfelt in old Doc's manner. His hands were strong yet comforting. He was a dying breed among doctors. He loved his work, was not wealthy and didn't care to be. He had never given anyone a bill unless he was sure they could afford to pay it.

Kemper, on the other hand, was young and disconcerting. Nick found him almost terrifying. His hands were soft, immaculate, kind of womanish; the husky college ring he wore fit the package perfectly. He was cold and analytical. His office was stark; the magazines in the waiting room were boring. Nick always got nervous sitting there, his hands clasped on his lap, apprehensive, fidgeting in anticipation of having to spend an entire half hour with him. He hated these visits, yet he *had* to endure them.

Every two weeks, for months now, Nick had attended sessions at Justine's request, riding his bicycle into town to Kemper's bungalow on Main Street. Though he despised any amount of time spent with Kemper, he did like being in town; it was the only time he ever *saw anybody*. It calmed him to watch people scurry around. They knew nothing of his pain; they weren't sick in the heart. They smiled and laughed; they seemed to lead regular, simple lives. Regular. Simple. Like his had been once.

For six weeks following his father's death, Nick never spoke. Not a word, not to anyone. He simply stared ahead, his eyes blank. After two weeks of that, he was placed in a psychiatric ward for observation.

That had been the most horrible time of his life, the week he spent there. He ate; he slept. But he never spoke. The doctors released him after seven days, telling his aunt that he seemed all right, that he gradually would return to normal. They felt his recovery would be quickened by sending him home.

Justine had her doubts. She was afraid the condition might be permanent and contacted Dr. Kemper.

All the while Nick knew what was going on, and he knew as well that he should behave and maintain at least a façade of normality. He ate when he had no appetite. He carried out his normal chores on the farm. But still, he talked to no one.

It took Kemper a long time to get the whole story, to understand why Nick did not speak. He talked to Justine, and to the police and other locals. Eventually he learned exactly what had happened.

• • •

Snow had been forecast, but when they got up that morning it was raining. By eight-thirty the temperature was dropping, and the cold rain fell hard and fast, leaving a blanket of water that would soon turn to ice. The snow followed. Nick sat in the living room near the stove heater, looking out the window, watching the countryside begin to turn white. Charles and Mary Lee had been gone only a couple of hours. Normally Nick would have accompanied them into town, but he hadn't been feeling well the night before, and a night's sleep hadn't cured him completely. He missed his parents whenever he was away from them, but he knew that they would return soon with their groceries and wood for the fireplace and a movie from the video store.

• • •

Later, when they pieced it together, they realized that the accident happened fast.

Mary Lee sat on the passenger side of the truck cab; Charles was driving. The cord of wood made the back end of the pickup extremely heavy, much more than Charles had figured. Plus the front wheels weren't properly weighted, and one bad bump could send the cab skyward.

The rain froze quickly as the temperature dropped, turning the roads into sheets of ice. Then the rain changed over to snow and a virtual blizzard ensued; four inches of snow fell in a little more than an hour. Realizing that conditions would only get worse, Charles decided to try and make it home, fearful that they would get stuck in town if they waited any longer. He was a good driver, and he drove carefully. But the defroster was broken, and he had trouble seeing. Both Charles and Mary Lee had to scrape the inside of the windshield as they drove.

The truck went into a sudden skid and moments later Charles was dead. Mary Lee was thrown free and stumbled around in the snow until she fell in the road, unconscious.

• • •

Justine was in her small apartment in Kansas City when the call came. The hospital in Hampton had gotten her number from Mary Lee's address book. Justine listened in stunned disbelief as she learned that her brother, Charles, her only sibling, was dead. The doctor asked her to fly to Ohio. Someone had to be with Nick.

Five hours later a highway patrolman met her at Hopkins Airport in Cleveland and drove her to Hampton. It was a very quiet hour-and-a-half ride through the still-falling snow.

At the hospital she was met by a social worker who explained that Nick had been sedated hours ago, and was still asleep. Mary Lee was in intensive care, alive but unconscious, fighting for her life. Two doctors reaffirmed that Charles was dead. A nurse held her as she cried.

"What can I do?" Justine said, through her tears.

"What can I do?" She wanted her brother to come back to life.

"You can help Nick," one doctor answered.

"He needs you," the other added. He touched her gently on the arm. "Someone has to tell him."

She asked to see Mary Lee first, to see her alive, to tell her she was there, whether Mary Lee could hear her or not. *Then* she'd see the boy.

She sat with her sister-in-law for two hours, holding her limp hand. She prayed, leaning forward on her chair, her forehead on the mattress. It was unreal, unthinkable, the whole thing.

At the reception area down the hall, Nick awoke, disoriented and angry. He demanded to know what was going on, why he was there.

A neighbor, Farmer Blough, had appeared at Nick's house that morning and, along with a sheriff's deputy, had driven him to the hospital. Nick knew that something was terribly wrong, and they told him that yes, there had been an accident. But when they reached the hospital, the doctors and nurses would only say that his parents had been in an accident and that they were in the hospital. Then someone gave him some medicine and he fell asleep.

Now, before anyone could stop him, he began combing the hallways, looking into rooms, looking for his parents.

Justine had almost fallen asleep holding her sister-in-law's hand, when she heard the door open. She sat up and saw a wide-eyed Nick. He'd found his mother.

It was a horrible moment. Nick stopped cold when he saw Mary Lee. He turned white, shocked at the sight; tubes were connected to her body, her hair was stringy, her skin bruised, her eyes black.

This, Nick thought, is what everyone's been hiding from me.

Then he saw Justine. Although he had never met her, he recognized her immediately from photographs. He ran toward her, practically screaming, "Is she all right? Is she all right?" Justine stood helplessly as he grabbed her by the arms and shook her, now yelling, demanding answers. Then he saw his mother again and he stopped.

He moved to Mary Lee's side and sat on the bed. He spoke to her, but there was no response.

"Nick, please, I . . ." Justine began.

"Let me stay with her," Nick said. "Just leave me alone with her for a while. Please."

The nurses looked at each other, then shrugged, silently agreeing it would be all right to leave him there if they kept an eye on him. Besides, it was obvious the boy's aunt needed a break.

The last nurse to leave turned back and said, "I'll leave you alone for a minute. Now don't touch anything."

Nick waited until her footsteps faded before he faced his mother. He looked at the needle in her arm, at the plastic tubes running to her mouth, at the skinny blue one in her nose. What are they doing to you? he wondered.

• • •

A nurse had just given Justine a drink of water when another in the nurses' station noticed that Mary Lee's remote heart monitor had beeped an alarm and the line had gone straight. Everyone rushed down the hall and into the room, where they found Nick pulling out the tubes and disconnecting the wires on his mother's body.

Justine finally asserted herself and pulled him out of the

room. "Let me go!" he screamed at her, twisting in her grasp so hard that two of her fingernails broke. An attendant came rushing to help her and Nick was finally subdued.

Suddenly the anger seemed to break. Nick's face relaxed and he put his head down and said nothing for a long time.

"I'm sorry," he said finally. "I'm really sorry. I'm glad you're here. Dad talks a lot about you." At that moment his eyes swung up and met Justine's for the first time.

He's a stunning boy, she thought in that second. His eyes, so intelligent. Piercing.

This was going to be the hardest thing she ever had to do.

He must know by now, Justine thought, but he would not bring it up. He *wanted* someone to tell him.

She would love a drink. Why hadn't she thought to stick a bottle in her purse? It would make all this so much easier.

She took Nick to the hospital cafeteria and bought him a cheeseburger and watched him eat it. She wanted him to get some food into his system before she broke his heart.

From personal experience Justine knew one thing about broken hearts—the appetite was the first to go.

Nick said nothing as he ate, keeping his eyes cast down. When he was done they looked over a crossword puzzle, but since they didn't have a pen, they just guessed the words out loud. Finally Justine said she thought a walk would be a good idea; Nick agreed.

The snow had stopped and it had turned colder. The crisp cleanliness of winter air hit their nostrils, and they stood for a moment, sucking in oxygen.

They had walked for less than a minute when Justine took a deep breath in preparation for what was to come.

Before she could speak, Nick said, "They haven't let me see my father yet. It's because he's dead." There was a pause. Then he said the rest, "Isn't he? . . ." Justine was already nodding. She reached to hug him, but he pulled away. Then he walked off, without a word, without any further reaction.

She watched him cross the driveway and sit on a bench. She retreated back into the warmth of the hospital and stood just inside the door, torn between a desire to hold the boy, and the realization that, for now, he needed his space.

An hour later Nick rose and ambled back inside, his nose bright red, the hair that framed his face frozen from the constant wiping of tears. He remained silent, then and all during the awkward drive back to the farm.

It would be over a month before anyone would hear the boy say another word.

• • •

During the weeks of his silence, Nick harbored resentment for Justine. Their first meeting, by his mother's bedside in the hospital, remained a barrier between them, a subtle obstacle that stood in the way of friendship. They got along, eating together, sharing responsibility. Although Nick wanted to look after his mother, taking her tea and coffee, covering her with blankets.

During this time Justine consulted with Dr. Kemper, the local psychologist, informing him of Nick's daily behavioral patterns.

Everyone was baffled by the boy's refusal to converse

with anyone. No one realized that during this extended period of silence, existing in a cocoon of his own making, he *had* been conversing, more and more as time passed. On Braves' Point.

Voices

NICK walked in Braves' Point meadow, his head tilted back, his eyes searching the vastness above him. The clouds, motionless puffs, hung white in the Ohio gray-blue sky. "You're bee-ootiful," Nick said as he spun slowly, his arms outspread.

He stopped suddenly, and looked about. "Are you there?" he said, calling out into the empty meadow.

"We are here," a voice answered.

Nick froze in place. For a few moments he listened to the sounds of birds and the pure white noise of wind and empty space.

"Do you know us?" a voice asked.

"Yes . . . you are the Erie dead. Husbands and wives, and all of their children, killed."

There was no answer at first, just the sound of the warm wind through the elm branches. Then a voice came, a different voice: "*How* do you know us?" it asked.

"You lived on these lands for thousands of years undisturbed until the Iroquois wars," Nick said.

"Yes. *All* of us . . ."

"Yes," Nick repeated, in total sympathy, "all of you."

"But *how* do you know us?"

"How?"

"Yes, how . . ."

Nick thought for a moment. "My father. He told me."

"What did he tell you?"

"That you were 'exterminated,' " Nick said, now understanding what exactly they wanted—to hear their story told. "And that the memory of you should never be lost."

"Yes," a voice said.

"Yes," said another.

And then another, and another.

Yes.

Yes.

Yes.

Nick collected his thoughts, trying to remember his father's words. He stretched his legs out, and ran his hands along them as he proceeded to recite the story as he remembered it. "Man has an evil side," he said, "one that is indes—im—indiscriminate and hateful."

He realized suddenly that he was nervous, that sweat was forming on his forehead. Unusual. Up until now, his visits with the Erie had been mostly simple, pleasant—and now, all of a sudden . . .

Placate them, he thought, just go on . . . "The evil part . . . of human nature, killed . . . the Erie. And we—I, must be careful not to let th—"

A voice interrupted. "It was genocide . . ."

"What?" Nick said. He knew the word.

"Genocide," the voice repeated.

"Yes," Nick said. "Genocide."

He slowly squatted, resting his arms on his knees, he hung his head down. How did the voices know that word? he wondered. They hadn't ever said it before. But Charles had, and Mary Lee had given him hell for it, claiming Nick was too young to be introduced to such dark realities. Nick remembered the "genocide" dinner, because afterward, even after Nick had gone to bed, his parents argued, something they hardly ever did.

Now, for the first time, the voices were speaking his father's words. Was it coincidence? He found in his memory something Charles had said on several occasions. "Man owns nothing," he said aloud to the meadow.

And just as quickly the voices took over: ". . . on the earth, no one owns the land; the land is God's, made ready for humans but not given to them."

And Nick joined in, and together the chorus of voices filled the air, but Nick's stood out, his the loudest voice of all.

"Even our house, and barn, and cornfields—they are all gifts that belong to a more powerful and gracious owner who at any time can reclaim them . . ."

And then he let the voices go on, by themselves, and he lay back listening to them, remembering . . . "the act of genocide is the greatest sin, the worst spiritual crime . . . erase the genetic line and you trap the souls; then the souls are caught outside, scratching to get in, separated from the living by only a filament—just close enough to make us remember, but unable to penetrate the veil that separates the un-dead from the dead."

The words seemed so familiar. For a split second he

actually thought he heard his father, heard the voice blending with the others. It was happening again—the sensation, like when the buck horn appeared fake, reality distorted in a few uncontrollable moments. Dizzy, almost nauseated, he called out, "Dad?"

Suddenly the voices stopped. There were no more that day.

The Ghost

"NICK, your father never knew what hit him. He never regained consciousness. There was no pain."

Nick stared ahead, noticing Dr. Kemper's nose hairs, in need of trimming. He reached up to his own nose, wondering if he had them himself.

"Nick?"

"Yes?"

"Did you hear me?"

"No," Nick said, not at all belligerently.

Kemper stirred in his chair. He tried a different approach. "Nick—do you feel angry?"

Nick slowly turned his head from side to side.

"How are all our friends in the Indian tribe?" Kemper asked, trying to be nonchalant.

"Fine."

"Have they given you any good advice lately?"

"Sure," said Nick, twisting sideways and hoisting his

leg up over the arm of the chair. "Buckeye season is just beginning. If you shine a buckeye with corn oil, and place it in your bed, it wards off evil. If you throw a buckeye into a river, a baby deer will be born. If a buckeye is—"

Kemper cut him off. "That's fine, Nick, that's enough. You can stop now."

Nick stopped talking and smiled. Kemper tapped his pencil on the desk.

"Nick . . . tell me. Why do you think you are here?"

For a moment, Nick was quiet. For a change, he was really considering the question. Kemper recognized the change and opened his eyes eagerly, looking at the boy over the top of his glasses.

"Because," Nick said, "everyone thinks I need help, because I went through a horrible tragedy. It's just the thing to do, for a young kid."

"So you think our meetings are a—preventive measure?"

"How's that?"

"In other words, there isn't anything wrong with you, but you come here to prevent anything from going wrong?"

"Yes. That's right."

"Look," Kemper said, "you tell me that you hear voices. You tell your aunt that you hear voices. Now, Justine doesn't hear any voices, and I think maybe you don't either."

Nick was not going to be tricked. He smiled. "I hear voices . . . I do." He wanted to drop his ace, to mention that old Doc Dugan had also heard them, when *he* was young, but decided to keep that bit of information up his sleeve.

"*That's* why you're here, Nick."

"Hmm," Nick grunted. Then he lashed out. "How much do you charge for my sessions?"

Kemper said nothing.

" 'Bout a hundred bucks?" Nick asked.

Kemper remained silent.

"And I've come here—let's see . . . been coming for six months, four times a month. . . . That's . . . four hundred times six, that's twenty—four, two thousand four hundred dollars! That's a lot of money. And I'm one client, and you must have what, twenty? Twenty times twenty-four hundred, that's—what is that? Do you have a calculator?"

Kemper just watched him.

"What would you do if you cured all your clients? You wouldn't make any money. Are you sure you don't just keep them dangling? Maybe even confuse them on purpose once in a while? Maybe even make them think they are sicker than they are?"

Kemper kept staring. Nick laughed out loud, half out of discovery and half at his own cleverness.

"Do you remember," Nick continued, "when I wasn't speaking to anyone? You promised that if I began to talk that you would cut my sessions down. Yet I still have to come every other week."

"I have to evaluate as I go along, Nick."

Nick knew what that remark meant. It meant that Kemper at any time could recommend he return to the psychiatrist for evaluation, and that ultimately he could end up in the hospital ward for observation. That had been the worst time of his life, being cooped up with crazies, playing with silly toys, staring out the ugly metal windows of the hospital.

Nick stood up and walked a slow circle in the room, looking at Kemper's degrees and pictures. His eyes stopped on a photograph of Kemper and his wife and two small daughters. "Those're your kids, huh?"

Kemper didn't answer.

Nick turned and looked at him. "Are they?"

"Mmm-hmm . . . ," Kemper answered, unwillingly. "Nick, I want to ask you one more thing today, and you don't have to answer me now. You can think about it until we meet next time."

"Like homework, right?" Nick said with a smile.

"Sort of," Kemper said, standing, collecting Nick's paperwork and placing it into a file folder. "I'd like to know if you ever feel—like *you* did something wrong . . . like your father's death was in any way your fault, or that you are guilty of *something . . .*"

Nick's smile faded. Was he talking about the shed? he wondered. Did he know about that? Justine, that's how he knows. She had told him.

It had crossed Nick's mind, at least once. He and Charles had had their first real falling out two weeks before the accident.

Then Nick burned down the shed. And then Charles was dead.

"Don't answer me now. Think about it," Kemper said.

The session was over.

• • •

Nick wheeled home on his Schwinn, frustrated by Kemper's question. He thought about the photograph of Kemper and family; they looked so happy, so *together*. He felt jealous of the two small girls; life to them must seem so simple.

Then he shook his head. No, he would not give in; he would not let Kemper get the best of him, he would not think about this anymore.

The mailbox at the end of the road to the farm was coming up fast. He veered to the gravel shoulder, preparing for a stunt he had practiced many times. He slowed just enough, then, as he passed the box, he thrust out his hand, and with a lightning-speed motion, snagged the mail out of the box without ever stopping.

He whipped into the farmyard, sliding to a stop just inches from the barn door.

He immediately heard the calves squealing inside the barn. Something was scaring them. He let his bike fall to the ground and ran inside.

The white cat stood above the stall, watching the cows and their calves, taunting them. The Jerseys mooed in protest as the cat walked back and forth on the rail. When it saw Nick, it darted off, disappearing into the depth of the barn.

Time for diplomacy, Nick thought.

He found a discarded container and skillfully extracted enough fresh milk from one of the cows to fill it up. Then he placed the milk on the rail where the cat had been, and moved quietly over to the barn door, where he would wait for the cat to take the bait.

A half hour later the cat emerged, made its way to the rail, and drank every drop. Nick watched until it was finished and cleaning its pure white fur, then announced his presence. "Hello there," he said, and the cat stiffened up, then darted away. Nick tried to follow it with his eyes, even walked to where he thought it had run, but it was nowhere to be seen. Vanished.

It was at that moment that Nick named him The Ghost.

• • •

The very next morning, upon waking, Nick was surprised to see The Ghost sitting on the window sill across from his bed, its eyes staring at him. *Hungry* eyes.

"Hey! The Ghost," Nick said very softly. He didn't want to scare the cat away; he wanted its company—any company at all. Suddenly that was incredibly important. He just couldn't bear to spend another day alone.

Nick didn't move for a long time. When he did get up, he moved slowly so as not to scare the cat off. He slid his pants on and made his way to the door. "I'll be right back. Wait here. Don't move," he said, and ran downstairs to get some milk.

When he came back The Ghost was gone.

He put the bowl on the window sill anyway and went outside to take care of his morning duties.

Once all the animals were fed he went to the garage and got out some fishing gear. He hadn't fished this summer since the rivers had warmed up.

And he had never been fishing alone.

He popped open Charles's tackle box. Immediately tears filled his eyes. Just the sight of the lures still in place as Charles had left them made him sad. He shut the box. He wouldn't take it.

He grabbed a single rod and hook and headed for the river.

• • •

When he was eight years old, Nick had been bitten by a dog in a shopping mall in Cleveland.

Charles had lived there when he attended his first year of college, before changing to Kent State; and though he still had friends in Cleveland, he rarely visited them, going back to the city only unwillingly, and for necessary business. It was on such a trip that a deceptively friendly looking Labrador bit Nick on the back of the leg.

He couldn't believe it at first, and he stared down at his torn pants; his leg didn't hurt right away, but it didn't feel normal either, and then he saw the blood. The pain came on, starting at nothing and growing into a constant throb, finally becoming so intense that he felt faint. He wasn't supposed to meet his mother for another half hour, so he told a security guard what had happened, and the guard had Mary Lee paged. Then Nick was transported to St. John's Emergency Room in downtown Cleveland.

Charles arrived within an hour and sent Mary Lee back to the hotel, and he sat with Nick. They were confined to a glass-enclosed waiting room. Then they were shown into a treatment room and a doctor came in. He cleaned the wound, wrapped it, then drew up an injection of antibiotics. Nick felt the cold steel pierce his skin, and looked up at his father, his eyes pleading: Can't you prevent this, Dad? Are you going to let this man stick his needle in me?

Charles sat with his hand on his son, trying to calm him

with words, but Nick noticed a terrified look on his father's face. "Cool down, Pop," he said in an effort to calm him, "I ain't gonna die . . ."

Since that incident, Nick had encountered dogs a few times, and each time a strange thing had happened to him: he found he couldn't move. His feet seemed to be frozen in place. He didn't *feel* as frightened as his body seemed to be—his mind was calm; he just couldn't move. Charles described what happened as a "syndrome" of some kind or other, and promised Nick that it would go away in time, and not to worry about it.

• • •

He wasn't a mile into the wilderness when he heard the whine of a dog up ahead. He saw it first in the distance, a dark figure running circles around something.

Nick stopped. He had to get around the dog. If he had to turn back and go a different way, it would take another hour to get to the fishing hole. So he eased alongside the woods near the river, but every path he chose seemed to lead back up toward the dog. Still he forced himself to go on.

Then it happened, and his first reaction was panic. *Not now!* he thought. *Not here!* Frozen in place just yards from the dog, all the memories of his earlier encounter, all the fears, swelled up from his subconscious. He looked down at his quivering knees.

The dog was black and scruffy, and wore no collar; it was obviously a stray. It took note of Nick's presence, staring at him momentarily, but then turned its head away —it sensed the boy's fear, and determined Nick was no threat. The dog was far more interested in something else, something trapped inside a hollow log. The dog tried to get into the different holes in the log, but his head was too wide. Frustrated, he snapped his jaws in the air and yelped.

Nick watched the dog closely. He remained frozen in place, yet mentally he plotted some way to help whatever it was trapped inside the log. He was certain it was an animal, probably a rabbit. And finally it was that—his concern for a helpless and frightened animal—that enabled him to move his legs, slowly at first, the first step more a shuffle. Then, as he realized his paralysis was broken, he moved more quickly, advancing with increasing confidence toward the dog.

It growled. Nick stopped. His legs would still move, but his palms were sweating, and his heart pounded. He backed off a few feet until he almost stumbled over a fallen limb. With a surge of confidence, he grabbed the large stick and advanced on the still-growling dog.

"Hey! Get lost!" Nick called out. "If you don't leave I'll have to hit you. I don't want to do it, but I will if I have to."

The dog seemed to pause for a moment, sniffing the air, assessing the situation. Where was the fear he had smelled before?

Still Nick stood his ground, his adrenaline pumping, his mind refusing to acknowledge the fear. This is what Charles would have done, he thought. He wouldn't have run away. Nick waved the stick at the dog, trying to seem threatening.

The dog couldn't have cared less. He sniffed the air again, then moved back to the log, never taking his eyes off Nick. Once more he growled at whatever was trapped inside. Then, apparently deciding that this was a battle not worth fighting, he turned and with a final growl trotted off into the woods.

Nick, his heart beating wildly, watched the retreating animal. Minutes after the dog was gone from sight, Nick remained frozen in place. A victory—not total perhaps, but a victory nonetheless.

Finally he relaxed and began to move again, making his way over to the log. He bent over and peered inside; he could see something in the very middle, silhouetted by the light from the other end. It appeared to be a small, shivering ball of fur, and judging by its size, Nick could tell it was a baby.

Surely it had been separated from its mother, Nick reasoned, surely it would die, unprotected in the wilderness.

Nick couldn't reach in with his hand, but in a short time figured out a foolproof means of catching it. He took off his sweatshirt and wrapped it around one end of the log. He took his stick and from the other side chased the animal out, into the sweatshirt, which he then gathered up. The animal tried to escape, cheeping in terror. That sound, and the minimal strength of the creature, confirmed that it was a baby and was harmless. Nick opened up the bundle and looked down upon a very young, very frightened squirrel. Its wide eyes didn't comprehend Nick's smiles, but after some moments the squirrel, having realized it was not going to be devoured, eased its struggle. Nick began the trek back to the farm, his new friend trembling inside the sweatshirt all the way.

• • •

Nick selected what would serve as the squirrel's home for the next few months—the now uninhabited rooster pen. It had plenty of hay and hiding places, enough room for it to scamper around in, and the fine-mesh wire that enclosed the area would both protect it from predators and keep it from getting away.

Before Nick set the squirrel inside the pen, he held it up to his face. "Hello, little fella. If you are a fella." He lifted it skyward and tried to check its gender, but wasn't at all sure what to look for in a squirrel.

"You're all right now, my little friend. You're safe," he said. "What do you like to eat, huh? Lettuce? Corn?"

He made his way to the food storeroom and took a can of corn, then cracked it open with an axe. He grabbed some cashews from an open tin and returned to the pen.

The squirrel nibbled the corn and then stopped, obviously not interested. Then Nick threw down the nuts and the squirrel ate all of them, then seemed to ask for more.

"Nutso, that's what I'll call you," he said, lifting the squirrel up once more. He touched its nose with his own. "Nutso. Boy or girl, no difference, that's your name." He left a bowl of water nearby and locked up the pen. He inspected the wire mesh to make sure there weren't any holes, and that the base was secure all the way round. "See ya, Nutso," he said, and turned toward the house.

Looking up toward his bedroom, he saw The Ghost sitting on his window sill. He felt suddenly elated to see the cat there—he felt it deep inside him, in his chest. In his heart. The very beginning of love.

A cat. And now a squirrel. Good company, he thought, and just what he needed, for there really was no one else.

No friend his own age. No father. For all purposes, no mother either. Doc Dugan was close by, but didn't seem to be the same old Doc lately. And Justine, the sad zombie, still in mourning and too often drunk—she was no company. Yes, the animals were simple, they would help him pass the summer; they were the perfect friends to have.

And no one could take them away.

July

NICK had little interest in television. Once in a while he would watch "The Simpsons," or the news, or a ball game, but rarely, if ever, did he spend an entire evening in front of the set. Like his father, he was an outdoor sort; Charles had shown him the glory of nature and the company it provides.

He could hear the TV going in the living room and went and sat with Justine during the network news. He had only seen five minutes of it when a report came on that really disturbed him.

An undercover federal agent, wired and carrying a hidden video camera, accompanied seven men in a boat on a trip off the coast of Alaska. As they came upon fifty or so walruses lounging in the surf, the men got out of the boat, walked to the water's edge, aimed automatic rifles at the unsuspecting herd, and opened fire. The walruses started dropping. As they were repeatedly hit by bullets, they moaned and screamed and looked around helplessly at their attackers.

Nick couldn't believe what he was seeing. The sight and sounds of the dying animals made him want to leap right through the TV screen to help them, to stop the hunters. He looked at Justine, who had her eyes closed and her ears covered with her hands.

Nick started crying and ran from the room. His tears didn't last long, but as he wiped his eyes he realized it was the first time he cried since he had sat on the bench outside the hospital on the day that his father died.

• • •

Later on, he sat in a chair across from his mother's bed. He still felt unsettled by the newscast. More for himself than for her he read the newspaper aloud. Afterward, he stared out the window—a wind had kicked up, and there was a smell, the smell before rain.

He hoped it would rain.

He fell asleep in the chair and slept there all night. Before leaving the room in the morning, he laid his ear on his mother's chest, listened for her heartbeat. He closed his eyes, remembering her as she once was, and said, "I'm not going to let you die, you know." He left her as he had found her, asleep.

• • •

At ten o'clock he met Arthur Digny at the mailbox, and the two talked for a few minutes. Then Nick walked back to the house with a new magazine and some bills for Justine. By all appearances, it was going to be just another normal day.

By its end, however, it would prove to be one of the most important days in Nick's young life. He was going to hear a voice he had never heard before.

The change was heralded by a storm, marching toward Sharon Lake, sending out thin scout clouds to announce its coming. Nick, once again setting out for the fishing hole, watched as long shadows fell when the clouds got in the way of the sun.

He walked a quarter mile before stopping at a row of pine trees. Once past there, his home would be out of sight. He turned and looked at the Harper farm—the house, the yard and barn, the fields that stretched for acres, the apple orchards. It had once been a kingdom to him; now it was only a place where time passed.

. . .

He stood at the bank of the river and threw a rock into the water, letting the image of his father's face come into his mind.

He threw another stone, and this time he heard his father's voice from deep inside his head. "Nick, you've got to read more. I'm tellin' ya. It puts your head in a space where there is no time, no limit, to what you can imagine. There's no place you can't go, there's no kind of person you can't meet. Anything that's known, you can know, too."

He threw a third stone and this time he thought of nothing. Thoughts of his father had to be used sparingly; they still hurt too much. Then he walked off toward the fishing hole.

Once there he rigged his line, pulled some cheese out of his pocket and put it on the hook, then cast his line into the water. He set it, getting just the right tautness. Then he sat on a log, and spread out the magazine he had brought with him. It was a *Car and Driver* magazine, one of the many Charles had subscribed to, and which kept coming. The twenty-four-valve engine on the front cover and the headline "Smart Engine" intrigued him. He went slowly through the article, thinking about what he was reading, going over the diagrams in detail. He was fascinated by the workings of a piston engine—something he knew nothing about. When he finished it, he closed the magazine and laid it aside, then stretched out on the grass. Slowly his mind emptied out, and he listened to his own breathing. And then the sounds of nature penetrated his consciousness—the river, still high from the heavy snows of winter and the rain showers of early spring, sloshed in a constant rush beside him. Soon Nick became hypnotized, wondering about the river and its secrets which churned and glided underneath.

He looked up. The sky had finished its change from blue to gray. Good, he thought as he heard thunder rumbling in the distance, I love rainstorms.

He could have tried to make it back to the farm, but instead he nestled under a thicket of bushes and pulled his coat over his head. Within a few minutes, the storm arrived and the heavens raged around him.

And after the rain, Nick gathered his fishing equipment and started back. The cow path on which he walked wound around, leading sometimes down to the river, other times up the banks, recessing slightly into the forest.

He came to an open area surrounded by a ring of trees. He could tell by the matted grass and remnants of fires and tent stakes that it had been used fairly recently as a camping spot.

He started to cross the space, but he couldn't walk any farther without going right through a large puddle. The storm had been heavy, he thought, to have created so large a puddle, and he stood looking at it for a few moments before deciding not to go splashing through it.

Then he heard it for the first time.

"Where am I?" a voice asked.

Had he heard it, or was he thinking it? He listened. It happened again.

"Where am I?"

That time Nick was *sure* he'd heard it. He backed up.

"Please. Help me," the voice said.

"Hello?" Nick said tentatively, not really expecting a reply.

"Hello," said the voice.

Nick was no stranger to voices, but this one was different. The others seemed to come from inside—inside his own head, body, soul, rather than from any *thing*.

This voice was distinctly coming from somewhere, and that somewhere seemed to be the puddle.

"Who are you?" Nick asked.

"I don't know," was the immediate answer. "Who are you?"

Nick walked the circumference of the puddle. He stopped, stooped, and looked at his own image in the water. "I'm Nick," he said.

There was no answer at first. He closed his eyes, listening . . . and finally the voice replied: "Hello, Nick."

Nick's head jerked in astonishment. He even smiled. "This is weird," he said.

"Isn't it?" the voice answered.

"Yes, it is," said Nick, quickly.

"It certainly is," replied the voice, just as fast.

Nick sat down. He had to get his bearings. He looked up, and around. Some birds were warring nearby. He could hear them screaming at each other. He could also hear the raindrops dripping, still draining from the trees. He knew those sounds were real; he knew where they came from. The voice had sounded as real and present as all those sounds.

"Do you know where I am?" the voice asked, its tone gentle, not demanding.

"I think so," said Nick, "you're a puddle of water."

"Water?"

"Yes, water."

"I'm confused," the voice said, "I was just—just—somewhere. I was . . . free . . ."

"Free?" Nick said.

"Free. Yes. Now, I can't move. I feel like I'm trapped." The voice grew anxious, and then stern. "Where am I? Why am I trapped?"

Nick swallowed. This was starting to scare him.

"Hello? Hello? Tell me!" the voice demanded.

Nick drew a deep breath. "Relax. It's okay."

There was a long silence. Nick could feel his heart pounding. He was frightened. He stood up slowly and began to back away, turning as he did. He considered the possibility that he had cracked, gone mad, or maybe this was *that word,* the one he had overheard at that terrible hospital he'd been put in—a *hallucination.*

"Hello?" the voice pleaded. "Are you there?"

Nick walked straight for the woods, picking up more speed with each step.

Then he ran as fast as he could. He could hear the voice, as it faded in volume. "You must help me! Hello! Are you there? . . ."

• • •

When Nick arrived home, he barked a hello at Justine and went directly to his room. He fell on his bed and just lay there, exhausted, confused. Relieved to be home, but haunted by a voice he did not know.

The Puzzle

NICK sat alone in his father's study. He had looked up the word "hallucination" in a dictionary, and then he read it aloud:

". . . False sensory impression lacking external stimulus or due to misrepresentation of actual external stimulus . . ." He then had to look up most of the words in the definition, and then most of the words in the definitions of the definitions, but eventually he figured it out. Most simply put, "hallucination" meant "seeing or hearing something that does not exist." It seemed to fit to a T the voice in the puddle.

His own father had told him of the legend of Braves' Point, that if one sits very still, it is possible to hear the voices of the valiant dead warriors. But the voice in the puddle was different—male; young; vulnerable. *And really there.*

Next he went to the encyclopedia for a broader explanation of the word: "Most psychiatrists consider hallucinations symbolic of repressed wishes . . ." Repressed wishes? Could that be it? he wondered.

Turning once again to the dictionary, he found the word "repressed": "Restrained, subdued, esp.: to exclude from consciousness."

He then looked up "restrained," "subdued," "exclude" *and* "consciousness."

What he pieced together didn't describe his situation at all. Certainly he wished—deeply—that his father were alive. But this desire was not "repressed"; on the contrary, it was foremost in his thoughts every minute of the day. He went back to the encyclopedia and continued reading:

". . . Some hallucinations are caused by emotional stress or great fatigue, for example, the imagined oasis of desert travelers." What about in dreams? he thought. Were they hallucinations? On many nights his father had come to him in a dream, seeming so real, his words of advice, his smile—and in the dreams, his father's hands still touched him, his lips still conveyed love. If a brain could hallucinate in sleep, it could probably do it when someone was awake, too, Nick reasoned. What was real, *who* was real? Nick just wasn't sure anymore.

He thought about the voice in the puddle. What could account for it? Nick felt normal. He didn't *feel* he was losing control. He didn't *feel* stress, or at least he didn't think so; he wasn't exactly sure what that was. But as far as he could tell, and aside from feeling sad and alone, he was fine. Besides, wouldn't Justine just come right out and tell him if she thought he was crazy? She was an up-front, no-bull kind of person, like his dad. Or was she choosing silence over getting involved?

He shook his head. What did all this matter? "When I go back, the voice won't be there," he said aloud, and left the study.

He thought of Nutso and got a can of peanuts from the kitchen and went out to the old rooster pen. Nutso was curled up in a corner. Nick undid the wire and slithered inside; he sat on the ground holding the squirrel in his lap. He admired this little animal—such a simple creature. It wanted food, it ate. It needed sleep, it slept. When awake it seemed content to just look around, sizing up the world. *That* must be the key to a happy life, Nick reasoned. Just look around.

The baby squirrel looked up from its food. It and Nick looked each other square in the eyes.

"What do you think, Nutso? You think maybe something's wrong with me?"

The Lost Glove

THAT night Nick had trouble sleeping. He kept thinking of the puddle, and of the voice. And of his father. There had been so many things he had wanted to say. If only he *could* have another chance. In particular, he wanted to talk about the fire.

November had been a cold but snowless month. Nick had looked eagerly toward his birthday, and on that day, November 22, Charles had taken him into Alliance to rent a videotape, saying he could pick out anything he wanted and keep it for the weekend. Nick spent a good hour searching through the selections and finally decided on the compiled edition of *The Godfather*.

On the way home they stopped and had lunch at the diner in Sharon Lake. They had a wonderful talk. Nick had loved it when Charles talked to him; he never felt talked down to. Mary Lee had said that Charles didn't really understand children, and that was why he talked to

Nick like he was an adult. Well, Nick didn't mind—he had liked it. At that lunch, Nick learned a lot about his father's earlier life, the time prior to his marriage to Mary Lee, and long before Nick was born.

"Do you know what a hippie is?" Charles asked him.

"No, not really," Nick said.

"The sixties . . . early seventies. People, kids mostly, grew their hair long, protested a war that was going on . . ."

"The Vietnam War," Nick said. "I learned about that in school."

"Right. Well, I protested against that war. Went to jail for it."

"Really?" Nick said. The image of his father in jail was hard to call up.

"I climbed on top of a war monument and spray-painted a peace sign on the flag. The flag on the monument. And they took me to jail for it."

Nick wasn't sure he really understood all this; he had always felt Charles was infallible.

He was about to find out differently.

• • •

Once home, Nick put the *Godfather* saga into the video machine and barely moved. Running time totaled six hours and Nick watched it three times in two days.

The following week at school, Nick was caught with a high-powered slingshot and a pocketful of "crackerballs" —small firecrackers that explode when thrown against the ground. Nick had been shooting them in the sling, and laughing with his friends as the small explosions peppered the concrete wall of the school.

Another student turned him in and the principal called him into her office. He told her his parents had given him permission to carry the slingshot. That was a lie. In fact, he had traded his baseball glove for the weapon and the firecrackers just that morning. The slingshot was by no means a toy. The handcrafted aluminum wishbone shaft and sight-scope gave *that* away, even to the principal, who had never seen a weapon quite like it.

She said she found it hard to believe that his mother and father allowed him to carry it, but because she knew him to be a well-bred and well-behaved boy, she gave him the benefit of the doubt. "Nick, if you bring me a note from your parents saying you are allowed to have this slingshot, you will not be punished."

Nick left when classes were over, walking home very slowly, figuring, trying to devise a plan to extract himself from the quagmire of his own lie.

He found Mary Lee in the basement, ironing. He presented her with a letter of permission that he had composed himself, and asked her to sign it.

"Absolutely not," she said without hesitation, "and where did you get that thing, anyway?"

"Mom, please. Please sign it. Please? This could mean disaster at school. She'll keep me—late. For weeks."

"No effin' way, Nick, and don't tell your father about it. He's in a bad mood as it is; his bank loan didn't come through, and he's not very happy about it."

Nick pleaded again. "Mom, I'm not gonna hurt anybody, I promise . . ."

"Except yourself, maybe."

"Mom, please sign it . . ."

"Look, Nick Harper, you told a lie. You're not fooling

anybody. Now you just go back to your teacher and tell her that you lied to her. Whatever the consequences, you'll have to deal with it. Now, go on upstairs, Nick. Now."

Nick left, frustrated. But a half hour later he returned, walked up to his mom, and said—quoting verbatim from *The Godfather* movie—"Look, Mom, *either your brains or your signature will be on this paper.*"

He was kidding, of course, although he had hoped to persuade her to change her mind. He could see from her expression, however, that he had made a terrible error. He did not expect her to react the way she did. Her hand went to her face and her eyes filled up. In that moment, it was as though they were total strangers. Nick felt instantly guilty, but it was too late. He had said it, and she was crying, and then she ran upstairs. He stayed in the basement for a while, embarrassed, sorry for having said what he had, but realizing the situation was beyond repair. He'd have to ride it out. Please, Mom, he thought, don't tell Dad.

But she did.

Charles was furious. Maybe the bad news on his bank loan was partially to blame, but he came down the basement stairs in an unprecedented rage. Nick couldn't believe it. Instinct told him to run, but he'd taken only a few steps when Charles caught him by the shirt and yanked so hard that he was pulled off his feet and fell backward.

Charles, of course, had no way of knowing that the shirt would rip in half. Nick left his father's grasp, was propelled into the air and landed against the furnace. Charles didn't see what happened; he had turned toward the stairway. And he was yelling too loud to hear the collision.

Nick's nose started bleeding immediately, and he sat for a few moments in shock before he started crying.

Charles had lost control. No loan when he needed it so much. He felt helpless. And add to that his son was turning into a Mafia Don.

He passed Mary Lee as he walked through the kitchen and threw her a glance, held up his hand in the air, imparting without words, Don't even *say any*thing!

But she had heard the noise and the crying. "What did you do? Huh?" she said, refusing to be bullied. "Charles? Just get out!"

Charles went to the safest place—the barn.

Mary Lee descended into the basement. When she saw Nick sitting on the floor holding his bloodied nose, she grabbed him, almost crushing him against her chest.

"He didn't mean it, he didn't mean it . . ."

And she held him, crying herself.

Then she took him to the bathroom, washed him up, put a cold towel on his nose and cradled him in her arms while he quietly cried.

Nothing was said by anyone for the remainder of the day. Charles kept his distance, waiting until Nick was in bed before even coming back into the house.

From his bed, Nick could hear them arguing. Mary Lee was completely on his side, that much he could make out. Charles still hadn't cooled down. "That goddamn kid will not talk to you that way, ever."

Up to that point there had never been a bad moment between Nick and Charles. Nick was devastated, and soon grew angry himself. He knew his shirt had ripped, and that his getting hurt was an accident, but by morning he was resentful, fortified by knowing that his mother would side with him, and that his swollen nose made him a pitiful sight.

If only Dad would come and apologize, he had thought. But he hadn't.

The next day was Saturday, and on Saturday mornings Charles always slept in. Nick didn't want to run into him when he did decide to get up, so he went outside with his slingshot hidden under his shirt and his pockets full of crackerballs. He had to hide them, otherwise he'd most certainly never see the slingshot again. If confronted, he would say he'd already given it back. Then, when the coast was clear, he would try for an even exchange on his baseball glove with the boy he'd traded with in the first place.

He went into the barn, but when he got there things changed. Unfortunately for him, he came up with what he thought was a brilliant idea, a little experiment that he could carry out before putting the slingshot away.

His father had left a five-gallon gasoline can by the door. It was almost empty.

Nick took the can to the shed and poured the few ounces of gasoline on the rear wall of the building, facing away from the house where no one could see him. Then he walked backward until he was two hundred feet away, so far that he could barely see the wet spot on the wooden wall. He loaded a single crackerball into the sling, stretched the rubber back to his cheek and lined up his target in the scope.

He hadn't anticipated success. He didn't really think it would work at all.

When the crackerball hit the gasoline spot, the shed wall

went up in flames like a smart bomb had hit it, and within ten minutes it burned almost completely to the ground.

Charles didn't even try to put it out. Instead he stood and stared at the fire, and at Nick, from across the yard. At that point he was not angry. He felt partially responsible; after a night's sleep and a lot of thinking, he felt terrible about what had happened the day before. So he took much of the blame on himself, and later in the day he apologized to Nick. He did ask for the slingshot, though, and Nick surrendered it on the spot.

But for weeks afterward there was a chasm between father and son, uncharted territory.

And then Charles was dead before all was forgiven.

The Middle of Nowhere

THE storm of a few days earlier had sent the summer season into high gear. The remaining pale shades of spring were replaced by the dark greens of late July. Nature, seemingly unaware of Nick's grief, forged ahead at its usual pace. As he stood at Braves' Point, a breeze kicked up, blowing across his face, playing with his hair.

"I heard another voice," Nick said.

There was no answer.

"Are there any of you anywhere else? Besides here, at your burial grounds?"

"No, we are all here," a voice rang out in response, as if it had been hovering, waiting.

"But are there others? In other places?"

There was no answer.

"You are all here? All the Erie?"

"Yes. We are all here. All the dead are here."

"I heard another voice," he said again.

And again there was no answer. The voices didn't always answer; he felt it best not to prod them.

He had risen early that morning and quickly finished off his morning chores, then headed straight for Braves' Point, avoiding the riverbank completely. He had a hunch that perhaps the Erie dead could help him identify the voice in the puddle. But the Erie didn't know anything about the puddle, and didn't care. In fact, he'd noticed that they were only interested in talking about themselves, and their own deaths, and the unjust manner in which their race was wiped from the face of the earth. Nick sympathized with them. Yet in spite of his respect for the Erie, he often found them irritating. They had no sense of humor. They never laughed. At times they repeated the same words over and over, and once Nick had to leave because their voices, hundreds of them, rose in a cacophonous swell of wailing and complaining. That had only happened once, but Nick never forgot it.

There was something really different about that voice in the puddle. And now, sitting on the Point, he was more certain of it. It had been a solo voice, the one in the puddle by the river, *one* voice. And it wanted help.

The Erie *never* asked for help.

And there was another thing that set it apart. To the best of his recollection, the voice in the puddle had spoken *first*. The Erie never did that. Nick, upon arriving at the Point, could sit for an entire hour and not hear a word, not until he opened up the conversation, not until he was willing to let them speak. Getting them to stop, however, was another question.

Yes. That's right, Nick thought, that puddle called out to *me*.

Suddenly he was shaken by a thought. The voice.

His father.

In a flash he was on his feet and gliding across the meadow. He descended the hill at full run. He stumbled at level ground, but kept going, racing as fast as he could toward the river.

Toward the voice.

• • •

When he saw the puddle he slowed to a walk. He noticed himself shaking a little, and he felt his breath coming in gasps. Many disjointed thoughts filled his mind as he approached. It's ridiculous, he thought; the voice won't be there. Hallucination. Hope. Fear . . .

"Hello," said the voice in the puddle.

Nick's eyes popped open in surprise.

"Hello?" the voice said again.

"Hi," Nick said as he neared the water's edge. He stood, waiting.

"I'm afraid," the puddle said.

"So am I."

There was silence for a while. Nick sat, wrapping his arms around his legs, resting his chin on his knee.

"Who are you?" the puddle asked, finally in the tense silence.

"I'm Nick. Who are you?"

"I don't know. I was hoping you could tell me that."

"You're—a voice, in a puddle, in the woods." He looked around. "In the middle of nowhere."

The puddle didn't answer right away. It seemed to be thinking. Finally it said, "A puddle? What is a puddle?"

Nick winced. The question seemed silly. "A puddle. Of water."

"A puddle of water?"

"Yes."

"Really?"

"Yes, really," Nick said, shaking his head, his tone implying that the puddle was less than brilliant. Certainly this spirit couldn't be his father. Charles was smart. Then what, or better, *who* was it?

It's much too lost, he thought, too confused to be an Erie Indian. Unless it is such a stupid one that all the others decided to throw it off the Point, and then it stumbled through the woods and fell into a puddle of water and got trapped there.

He had to ask. "Are you an Indian? A dead Indian?"

"What's an Indian," it replied, and Nick broke out laughing. He began to circle the puddle.

"You know what? Sometimes I think—no more voices. Just don't—*hear* them. And after meeting you, I'm really leaning that way . . ."

"What are voices?"

"Oh, my God!" Nick yelled, and fell down as if he had fainted in shock. "A voice, asking what a voice is!"

But now, lying flat out on the ground, with his arms and legs stretched out, he noticed something. He was relaxed. Though the puddle's stupidity irritated him, he no longer feared it. He could feel his muscles loosening, and his head felt light, as though he had cleared it of some dark and difficult things. He liked this new feeling, and lay there for a long time.

Finally he spoke, more to himself than to the puddle: "And I thought you were my father."

• • •

Nick lay next to the puddle for an hour, floating somewhere between sleep and consciousness. Then he heard a distant noise, the hum of Farmer Blough's tractor. It was getting closer.

Nobody liked Blough. He was a gruff old man who never laughed or smiled, who was bitter about life, and was always complaining, about any and every thing. The only person who'd ever even given the man the time of day was Charles. He'd looked in on him once in a while, and occasionally had sought his advice about farming. But the old man was so unpleasant that no one, not even Mary Lee, could understand why Charles bothered to keep Blough company.

Blough had come to Charles's funeral and had made everyone uncomfortable, chewing tobacco and spitting during the graveside service. The majority of the people there had been Charles's friends from college; they arrived in their shiny city cars. Blough rolled into the cemetery on his tractor. After the priest prayed over the coffin, everyone in turn, going around in a circle, said a few words about Charles. Blough was last, and Nick could feel that no one wanted him to speak, but Blough wanted to, and he did.

Oddly enough, of all the people there, Nick liked Blough's words the most.

But the guy still scared him and he never sought out Blough's company. They just came across each other once in a while.

"Shh," Nick said to the puddle as the tractor neared.

Blough pulled up and stopped, leaving the tractor at an idle. "Nick," he said, nodding.

"Farmer Blough, how ya doin'?"

"How's yer ma," Blough said.

"Mmm—fine. Same. Not so good, really."

"I got a little job fer ya, on my farm. If ya come by, it'll earn ya a few dollars. You're about old enough to git to workin', don't ya 'spect?"

The last thing Nick wanted to do was to be around Blough for any length of time. "Doing what?" he asked.

"Dig a couple of horseshoe pits."

Digging—that didn't sound so bad. He had done it before, when Charles was laying a water pipeline to the barn. Nick remembered the feeling—the shovel, sinking into the soil, pulling up the dirt, throwing it into a pile, trying to imitate his father's ease, and sleeping at the end of the day, so deeply.

"Sure, I'll do it. Sure."

"You come by when you're ready. Diggin's a good thing. Git the demons out . . ." Blough said, and for a fraction of a second Nick thought he saw the old man smile, something he was not known to do, ever. It was a little spooky.

Blough revved his engine, thrust the gearshift into first and rolled off into the woods without a good-bye.

"He's gone," Nick said to the puddle.

The puddle picked up right where they had left off. "Could you please describe what I look like?"

"You're kidding, right?" There was no response. Nick sighed. "Okay. You're round, sort of. And your water is about ten feet across. You're a puddle, you know, not a river, or a pond, but a puddle. You fell, from—the sky."

"Falling . . ."

"What?"

"Falling. I remember falling. Everything was one way; I was light. Free. Then everything changed."

"Yes," Nick said, "that's right."

"I'm trapped, now . . ."

"Yes, you are. But, um. . . . at least you're somewhere. Everybody's gotta be somewhere."

"Where was I? Before, I mean. I remember . . . I remember . . ."

"You were rain."

"Rain?"

"Yes, a few days ago it rained, and that's where you came from. Rain. Falling water."

"Yes, falling . . . and I remember rivers, and trees and small creatures, and how wonderful they are . . . *were* . . ."

"That's interesting," Nick said, "that you remember those things. They're still here, you know, it's just that you can't see them."

"Are they still . . . wonderful?"

Nick looked around, at everything. It was a difficult question. "I don't know."

"Why am I sad?" the puddle asked suddenly, totally out of context.

"Are you sad?"

"Very."

"About what?"

"Things, before I fell, I remember them. They were good. I want things to be like the way they were before."

Nick let his head fall and said, "I understand."

He made his way home slowly, feeling better for having confronted this new voice. It really was unlike all the others. Maybe I can help it, he thought; I'd like to. The puddle did something to me—for me. I feel better, somehow, but I don't know why . . .

His thoughts were interrupted. There was the black dog, ten feet away, standing stiff-still. When Nick saw it lower its head, and when he saw the tail go down and heard a menacing growl come out of its mouth, *it started to happen again . . .*

The "syndrome," Nick thought. My legs. I can't move them. The dog remembers that I threatened him—he must! Now he's going to get me. I've got to break this thing.

Much to his surprise, however, the dog did not attack. Instead it turned and jaunted off, tail between its legs. But not without a parting growl.

At that moment Nick was glad he was alone, that no one was there to see him stuck in the mud, unable to move. Only after the dog was completely out of sight did his ankles and knees loosen enough for him to head toward home.

Obviously he and this stray dog were inhabiting the same territories. And in time, they would meet again.

Something had to be done about the dog.

The Home Plate Kiss

THE dream was deeply disturbing at first.

Something terrible had just happened. He was at school. People were running and screaming, lives were in danger.

When the excitement had started, Nick had been in class, sitting across from Pam Sue Healy. Thinking of what his dad would have done, he'd grabbed her hand and had led her through the danger and chaos to the safety of the basement. Once there they sat together, shivering; she was crying. Nick noticed she was all dressed up, like for a party or something. Then she stopped crying and was staring at him. At first he was embarrassed, but then he noticed that her deep blue eyes were not only grateful, but admiring. She held his hand, the hand of her savior, and leaned up and kissed him on the mouth. It was wet and wonderful.

He woke up.

And as if overnight, Nick became conscious of girls. It was that time in his life, the moment of awakening.

He closed his eyes, trying to recapture the moment. He wanted to feel her touch again. His dad had told him that there would come a time when he would want to spend time with girls. Nick had found that hard to believe, but Charles had said, "Just wait." Could this be what he had in mind? Nick wondered.

He sure would have liked someone his age to talk to, but living out in the country meant seeing other kids only when he was in school, or when he went to town. Maybe he could call Pam Sue. But first he had to get up.

The Ghost sat in the window. It let out a meow.

Nick smiled. "Hey, The Ghost," he said. Just that quickly the cat disappeared, having jumped out the window and down onto the roof. Nick ran over and leaned out and they looked at each other.

"I'll get you some food," Nick said, and ran out of his room and down to the kitchen.

By the time he returned with a plate of food the cat was nowhere to be seen. He left the plate on the window sill, part of what had become an apparent ritual of feeding The Ghost: leave the food; the cat eats it when no one is there.

He returned to the kitchen and sat with Justine at the table. They talked about things, the usual morning talk. But Nick found he couldn't get Pam Sue Healy out of his mind.

Why?

He had known her since the third grade, when her family moved to Sharon Lake Township. As the new student in the class, and easily the prettiest, she had caught Nick's eye immediately. After a while, she seemed to notice him, too—looking back over her shoulder and smiling, coming to his rescue when he needed a pencil or paper, letting him in line in front of her and so on, and though he was flattered that the prettiest girl in school paid him this much attention, he was much more interested in other things to take it seriously.

Then something had happened this past May, just before school had let out for the summer. Pam Sue had attended an all-night pajama party with some of her friends. One of the girls had brought along some beer, and all the girls stayed up until morning, giggling, laughing, and talking—mostly about boys and sex.

Two of Pam Sue's friends extolled their own promiscuities. Everyone gathered in a circle, and when it was their turn, they had to do the same.

As Nick heard it later, the girls gathered in the circle and each had to recount her most exciting experience with a boy. A couple of girls—who Nick knew from rumor might have been telling the truth—claimed to have gone all the way with guys from high school.

When it was Pam Sue's turn, she apparently tried to get out of saying anything, but when finally forced to confess to something, she told a lie.

She made everybody promise not to tell, then said that she and Nick Harper had almost gone all the way, but that she had finally refused him and he had gotten real angry.

Nothing was said of the confessions the next day at school. But on the following day it got back to Nick.

Nick was confused when he heard what Pam Sue had said. Why would she say that? he wondered. Sure, they had been friendly, and he thought she was easily the prettiest girl he had ever seen, but he really didn't feel like he knew her very well. They'd never even held hands. Yes, Nick decided, all this was confusing, but he really didn't care what the other kids said. Nothing like that mattered anymore.

When he first saw Pam Sue after the story of her confession got out, Nick could tell that she was embarrassed. Charles and Mary Lee had always told him to be tolerant of others, so he decided to try to help ease her discomfort. Besides, he really did want to get to know her better.

Pam Sue was surprised to find that Nick wasn't even angry. He asked her if she would like to take a walk on the baseball field.

They strolled through left field, trying their best to ignore a small gaggle of kids who seemed to be in pursuit. They were silent, except for a few outbursts of laughter. Then someone whistled the "Wedding March," and there was a bust of hooting and running in circles and high-five slapping.

Nick rolled his eyes. "Don't even listen to those buttheads. Look," he said, putting his arm on her back and leading her down the third base line, "this is really no big deal. And if I'm not worried about it, why should you be? Now let's just change the subject for a minute. See if that works. Okay?"

"Sure," she said, grateful at the ease he was showing.

As they arrived at home plate, they chatted about where they lived, what they'd done in the summer. Nick saw that she had relaxed some, yet he didn't want to lead her on. He figured he probably never would marry. Since losing his father, he had decided that he wanted to be independent, to not need anyone to depend on, and that included girls. Even very pretty ones like Pam Sue.

Nick looked at her, dismayed to see more and more kids collecting in the bleachers. They were cracking jokes and whistling, and making fake smooching noises.

Jerks, Nick thought. Screw 'em.

In a swift motion he grabbed Pam Sue, pulled her to him, and kissed her. At first her arms waved about in surprise, but, getting into the moment, she slowly raised them and wrapped them around his neck. The other kids fell into silence, and then broke into applause.

After what seemed an eternity, the kiss ended, and Nick and Pam Sue turned to the crowd and took deep bows.

• • •

For Nick, the home plate kiss had been more tactical than born of romance. Now, months later, as he sat staring into his cereal, the event rushed back into his brain.

A delayed reaction. He could think of nothing else but that kiss, that girl, well into the afternoon. Something had awakened in him, something that had been dormant, but that he sensed had always been there.

• • •

He spent the rest of the day wishing for night, thinking only of going to bed and maybe dreaming again of Pam Sue Healy.

After the sunset, with flashlight in hand, he checked on all the yard animals. Lastly he made his way to the rooster pen to visit Nutso. The little critter was growing fast; once it had fit in the palm of a hand; now it took both hands to hold it. The squirrel's snout was no longer pug, but noticeably elongated. Its hair was grown in full and its temperament different—no longer fearful, no longer studying the world, but existing in it. And Nick figured that he soon would have to return it to the wild.

When he hit his room he fell on the bed. He had almost drifted off to sleep when he smelled something strong, like—cat food. He popped up and looked at the window sill.

The Ghost's food. It hadn't even been touched.

That had never happened, not once.

Every Other Thursday

THE words came out of Dr. Kemper's mouth slowly; they seemed to take forever.

"So, how're things going, Nick?"

Wow, Nick thought, that's a loaded question. Do I tell him anything? Heck no. "Things are fine," he answered, and smiled.

Kemper didn't believe him. "Indians? Since we last met?"

"Mmm-hmm . . ."

"What did they talk about?"

"Oh . . . things . . ."

"What kind of things?"

"They're mad . . ."

"Why?"

"Because they were . . . killed. Murdered."

"Some pretty dark topics, Nick."

"Dark?"

"Dark. Um, dark . . . I don't want to say evil, but you know, not good . . . not *light,*" Kemper said, holding his arms up in the air as if holding a sunbeam, "but dark . . ."

"I'm not sure what you mean."

"Gloomy. Sad."

"Oh."

They sat for a moment, saying nothing.

"I forgot the original question," Nick finally said.

Kemper shifted in his seat. "We'll start somewhere else. How is your mother doing?"

Nick glanced at the floor. "She's—the same, not well. I haven't spent too much time with her lately."

"And why not?"

"Things have been a little busy."

"Busy? You usually talk about how there's nothing to do . . ."

"Yes. I know. I don't know the answer to your question. Just that a lot of things have been on my mind."

"Your aunt tells me you've been spending a lot of time in the woods, alone."

"Well, yeah. Been doing some fishing." Nick rolled his thumbs. Kemper saw it.

"And talking to Indians?"

Nick nodded, saying very matter-of-factly "Yeah." Be cool, he thought, answer the questions. Be normal. But what is normal? Who am I convincing, Kemper, or me? He sees through me . . . he knows.

"Nick?"

"Yes?"

"Are you all right?"

Beautiful Eyes

ANOTHER day and night passed and Nick didn't see The Ghost anywhere. He went to bed worried, even had trouble sleeping. The next morning, when he awoke, the cat was in his bed, curled in between his legs.

At first Nick was delighted at the unprecedented visit. He reached down to pet the cat, but as he ran his hand over its white fur, its body felt warm to the touch. He gently picked it up and held it with his arms crossed underneath. It seemed totally listless. Its watery eyes looked distant, glazed. "Oh, God," he said, "'smatter, Ghost?" He rocked it in his arms for a while, then laid it down and covered it. The normally skittish Ghost offered no resistance.

Justine came up to have a look at him.

"It's got a flu or something, Nick."

"Yeah, somethin'."

"You oughta take him on into the vet. Can you get him there on your bike?"

Nick nodded. "I can figure a way," he said as he sat on the bed and stroked the cat.

"He'll get better, Nickie. He's probably never had any shots, you know?"

"Yeah," Nick said, nodding, unconvinced.

• • •

Nick sat in the barn, wiring a plastic milk crate to his handlebars. "This is *all* I need," he said aloud, "a little more illness; c'mon, let's pile it on, let's pile it on . . ."

When the crate was secured, he padded it with straw, then carried The Ghost down from his bedroom and placed it inside. He inverted a cardboard box and placed it on top to prevent the cat from escaping.

He pedaled his one-speed Schwinn out onto Stanepote Road and headed for town. The weight of the crate and cat made it difficult to climb the small hills. Halfway through the journey he took a rest.

He stopped at the intersection of Stanepote and Route 534 and parked his bike under a large green sign that read "Welcome to Sharon Lake" in white letters. Printed under those words, in much smaller letters, was "Sharon Lake Township. Population 1140." He checked on The Ghost, whose eyes asked, What the hell are you doing, but it hadn't the strength to protest too much. Nick tried to comfort the cat as best he could with soothing words. "We're taking you to the doctor, Ghost. We're gonna make you better. Okay? You okay?" He petted him for a while, then sat back on the ground, leaning his back up against the road sign.

He just sat for a while, in that spot.

Once in the small village of Sharon Lake he found a welcome sight: people bustling about, standing and talking, laughing. He cycled past them, and past buildings that jarred memories, like the hardware store, where he and his father had spent lots of time; the goods store—everyone knew Nick there. All the places reminded him of Charles, but he saw before him proof that the world just went on anyway.

He pulled up to the animal hospital, parked his bike and carefully extracted The Ghost from the crate. He went inside, feeling a little nervous.

He approached the desk. A kindly woman greeted him. "Hello, there . . . ," she said.

"Hi," he replied, "um, I'm Nick Harper . . ."

"Yes," she said, cutting him off, "and that must be Ghost."

Nick blinked. He couldn't imagine how the lady knew the cat's name. "*The* Ghost," he said, correcting her.

"Oh, *The* Ghost, I see," she said, as she got out the blank forms for Nick to fill out. "You haven't been here before, have you, Nick?"

"No. Um, excuse me, but how did you—his name?"

"Your aunt called."

"Oh . . ."

"Have you been here before, Nick?"

"No, but—does Dr. Jergen work here?"

"No, he doesn't, but we know him . . ."

"Oh, 'cuz he used to come out to the farm, when we had more animals, and when"—he swallowed and looked her straight in the eye—"when my father was alive . . ."

She already knew the story. Everyone in Sharon Lake did. "I know, I know . . . I'm sorry, Nick."

There was an uncomfortable moment. Nick looked at his cat and changed the subject. "He's not doin' so good, The Ghost."

"Well, the doctor will take care of him, Nick, don't you worry."

Nick knew better than to have blind trust. "We'll see, huh . . ."

"Just take—*The* Ghost into Room One there, and the doctor will be with you in a minute."

Nick went into the examination room and stood in what he found to be a cold, unfriendly place. Hard metal table, bottles, syringes and cotton balls. He whispered into The Ghost's ears, trying to comfort him. When the vet appeared, Nick recognized the man instantly. From the burial. One of the people standing over the hole in the ground . . .

"How are you, Nick?" the vet said, putting one hand on Nick's shoulder.

"M'okay. Fine," Nick said. "You knew my dad, huh . . ."

The vet looked at the floor, blinked, then looked back into Nick's eyes. "Yes. I did."

Nick nodded. "I remember you."

"You—doin' okay, Nick?"

Nick got the drift. What the vet was *really* asking was, How are you handling life since they dumped your old man's body into that hole?

"Um—I'm fine," he said slowly, "thanks for asking. But I'm not here for me. I'm here for The Ghost."

"Right, right . . ." the vet said, as he lifted the cat from Nick's arms. "Let's see this guy."

All attention shifted to The Ghost, and Nick felt instantly better, as if The Ghost were already on his way to recovery. "Where'd you get him?" the vet asked.

"Well, he just sort of showed up at my house. You know, hung around for a while, then I started to feed him, and before you know it, he was—my cat."

"Handsome fella," the vet said, as he stretched The Ghost's mouth open and looked at his gums. Then he grabbed the scruff of its neck, pulled it, and watched it fall. "He's a little dehydrated. Has he been eating?"

"No. Not in two days."

"Drinking water?"

"I don't know. He drinks out of the cow trough. So who knows—hard to tell."

"Hmm," the vet said. He grabbed an anal thermometer and inserted it into the cat.

"Ooh," Nick said, speaking for The Ghost.

After a minute, the vet read the temperature aloud. He said it was a little high. He prepared two injections and shot them into the scruff of The Ghost's neck. He gave Nick a bottle of liquid medication and showed him how to administer it.

"It's probably a bacterial infection, Nick. Just keep an eye on him and if he doesn't improve in a few days bring him back in."

"Okay."

"Can I ask you something? Why did you name him The Ghost?"

"He appears and disappears. Right before your eyes."

"That's cats," the vet said.

Nick lifted The Ghost and carried him out to his bicycle and put him in the crate. He wheeled carefully out into the street and slowly eased down Main.

. . .

It was good to see so many people. Some of them he knew, but he avoided eye contact with them. If he stopped to talk, they would all say the same thing—Sorry, Nick, are you all right?

He was content to think of his father as he rode along. As he passed the train-car diner, he noticed it was empty, and decided to go in. He'd worked up a thirst.

The booths, which had once seemed so friendly, now looked ominous and mocking. He didn't want to sit in one of those, as he and his father had, so many times. In fact, he wondered why he had come in at all, and probably would have left right then if the waitress hadn't snagged him.

She saw him staring to the booths. "You can sit in one of them if ya wanna."

"No; a stool. I'll sit here," he said as he sat.

"What can I get you?"

Nick only had about a dollar. The waitress handed him a menu. Except for beverages, everything cost well over a dollar. Nick's eyes set on "coffee . . . 50¢." He ordered that, and a glass of water.

The waitress blinked. "Well if that's what you want. I'm making a new pot, can you hold on a minute?"

"Sure."

Nick sat for a while in silence. He clasped his hands on the counter in front of him and rolled his thumbs. Then he spotted a newspaper a few stools down, shuffled sideways and retrieved it. He checked the classifieds for lost pets, thinking there might be a description of the black dog, but there wasn't one. He skimmed the front page but found nothing of interest, so he folded the whole mess up and set it on the stool next to him. He put his head down on his forearms, suddenly feeling depressed—the diner was not his favorite place anymore. Then he heard the glass doors open and he spun sideways to see who was coming in.

He felt his heart sink. Of all the people he should run into, he never expected it to be the girl he'd been dreaming of.

"Hi, Nick," Pam Sue said.

"Hi, Pam Sue," Nick said. She looked even prettier than he remembered. But when he saw her mother follow her in, he felt flustered and suddenly very shy. He immediately spun on his stool so he was facing the grill. He now wished he hadn't ordered the coffee. Otherwise, he could just leave. Just then the waitress came over and placed a cup down, and filled it, and he knew he was stuck.

He figured if he sat in silence, he could drink up quickly and leave. He grabbed the coffee, not accounting for the near-boiling temperature, and took a gulp. The heat seared his tongue. He spit a mouthful back into the cup, hoping that Pam Sue hadn't seen it happen. Careful, he thought. Drink up and bolt.

But then he heard Pam Sue's voice. "Momma, this is Nick."

He had no choice. He had to turn around. "Hi," he said to her.

"Well, hello, Nick," Mrs. Healy replied. Pam Sue

smiled brightly at him, and for a brief instant he felt something melt inside.

"Come join us, Nick," Mrs. Healy said.

He felt a little sick. He looked out the window at his bicycle. The Ghost was most likely asleep, but he could use the cat as an excuse to leave at the earliest opportunity. He moved to the booth, leaving his coffee at the counter. Pam Sue moved aside to make room for him.

"Would you like to have some lunch with us?" Pam Sue asked.

"Um, no, no, I've got some coffee over there . . . ," he answered.

"You drink coffee?" Pam Sue said, amazed or impressed—he wasn't sure which.

He slid his eyes to the left. He wanted to answer her, but her eyes locked onto his, and he could think of nothing at the moment.

"Aren't you going to get it?" Pam Sue asked.

"What?"

"Your coffee . . ."

"No. It's too hot."

Pam Sue and her mother exchanged glances. Then Pam Sue leaned sideways and knocked him with her shoulder, trying to loosen him up. She was so close to him that he could smell a scent. Something was happening to him; his senses were going wild. Still he tried to act nonchalant, which he did with mild success.

"So you two go to school together," Mrs. Healy said, more as a statement than a question.

Pam Sue answered. "We've been in the same class—since we moved here, Mom."

"Yes," Nick added, "the same class." He definitely had to make an escape. But how could he do it politely?

He could feel Pam Sue looking at him, but he stared across the table at her mother. She talked, but he didn't hear her. Every few seconds, he would glance to his left and catch a glimpse of Pam Sue. Then he looked away.

Mrs. Healy went on, but still he couldn't make sense of the words she was saying. He hoped that she didn't ask him any questions because he had no idea what she was talking about. His heart felt like it had flopped over, and a glorious tingle went from the base of his spine all the way up to the top of his neck.

Then it was all over. Too soon. They left so suddenly, it seemed.

He turned and looked for them outside, but they weren't there. He closed his eyes and wished that he could meet up with Pam Sue again soon. Then he went back to the counter, where his coffee sat, cold, un-drunk. He sipped it. It was awful.

The waitress saw him push the cup away. She sauntered up to him. "You okay, kid?"

"Huh?" he said, as if coming out of a trance. "Yes. I'm fine. Thank you." He stood up.

"You know, sonny, you've got beautiful eyes," she said.

"Huh?"

She smiled. "Fifty cents," she said.

"Oh, right . . ." Nick fished three quarters out of his pocket and placed them on the counter. "Thank you very much," he said, then turned and walked out the door.

• • •

The waitress watched through the window as he mounted his bike and pushed off and turned a large circle in the street. Her fingers crept over to the coins on the counter and she slid them into her hand, and dropped one quarter, her tip, into her apron pocket. A tip, she thought. From a kid.

Falling

JUSTINE loosened her blouse just enough to dab her breastbone with a towel. Then she pulled a small fan over to the bed and sat in front of it for a while. Opening the drawer of her bedside table, she pulled out a small pipe, lit it, and took a puff of marijuana. Finally she lay back on the bed and closed her eyes, wondering where she had gone wrong, why she was alone, why the world had grown so unfriendly; and she hoped that Nick didn't know how she saw him only in a haze, through the wine in her eyes, and she felt guilty, because she couldn't get out of her own sadness long enough to *really* love him.

She had chosen not to drink any alcohol for a few days and was having a tough time of it. It was six o'clock and she noticed her hands shaking; her blood longed for its familiar friend.

If only there were a good bar to go to, she thought, where she could sit and talk with someone, anyone. She missed her friends in Kansas City, but didn't miss Kansas City. Life there had been one disappointment after another, and the last one had nearly done her in. She felt so old—she would turn forty-three soon and the thought horrified her.

She got up and walked to her dressing table, sat in front of the mirror and looked at her face. Not a bad face, she thought, a little overweight and wrinkling around the eyes, and there were those two lines that dropped from her nose to the corners of her mouth, but her eyes were still pretty, and her lips full, and she had great hair. Still she wondered what good it did her, sitting in a farmhouse in the middle of Ohio.

One glass, she decided finally. One glass of good red wine. That, of course, turned into two, and by the time she had the dinner on the table she was temporarily happy. She called upstairs to Nick but he didn't answer. She went up to find him.

She poked his bedroom door open; only The Ghost was there, curled up in bed, exhausted from its illness and its trip to town. She figured Nick must be in his mother's room. She walked quietly down the hallway and stopped at Mary Lee's door. She could hear him singing—it sounded so sweet that she didn't want to interrupt him. She knew that if he was experiencing peace of mind, regardless of the means by which he achieved it, it was a good thing. So many times she had watched him, sitting alone in the yard for hours, and there was nothing she could say. Only time could heal him.

If only she could get close enough to help him.

She tapped on the door and the singing stopped.

"Yes?" came his voice.

"Got some dinner on."
"Okay, be right there."

• • •

That night the heat was unbearable. After dinner, Nick and Justine sat in the living room. Nick turned on the air-conditioner—something rarely done because of the cost of electricity. Confined to the only cool room in the house, they experienced a rare closeness. Justine was now well into her cups, so she was easy, and when Nick insisted that they not have the TV on, she agreed. Instead, they went through family pictures.

That night, Nick got a lesson in his family history. It was soothing, somehow, to leaf through the hundreds of photographs of grandparents, great-grandparents, uncles, cousins and friends of the Harper clan. Most of the people were now dead or moved out of the fold. Yet the world went on, the new generations replaced the old. Death was just a small gear moving as part of the large machine.

Nick saw features in his kin—a nose here, eyebrows there—that he recognized. He felt a part of them all. Even staring at pictures of his father, set against the many Harper dead, did not cause the usual pain.

If only he could hold on to that state of mind, when each single ingredient of the world around him made sense.

He glanced from a photo of his grandmother and then looked at Justine's face. He saw it. The Harper look. And in it, he saw a bit of himself.

As they put the albums away, Justine began to cry lightly. Nick comforted her, put his arm around her. At that moment, for the first time, he felt something truly special for her; he saw that they were *related;* she was a piece of him, a piece of Charles, and suddenly he felt lucky to have her.

Long after Justine was in bed, Nick was still awake, feeling the temporary strength, reveling in his ability to shake, if only momentarily, his omnipresent sadness.

. . .

In the morning The Ghost looked a little better; he'd eaten a small bowl of dry food during the night—the first time he'd eaten in three days. Nick held him up, nose to nose; The Ghost's eyes seemed brighter, less glassy. Nose cold —a good sign.

He raced downstairs and greeted Justine with an uncharacteristic kiss and the good news. "The Ghost is getting better!"

. . .

It was a bright, hot day. Bugs, all kinds, moved everywhere in their crazy circles. It seemed the rains had passed for a while. Somewhere hiding in the cloudless sky the locusts swarmed, their sound swelling and fading over the fields. The blistering sun and all the elements of nature, in unison, called out to Nick, giving him a message, beckoning him into the woods.

. . .

"I've been thinking," Nick said, not exactly sure how he was going to say what he wanted to say. "You are the strangest spirit I have ever encountered. You are the only voice more confused than I am. All the others, all of them—"

The puddle interrupted. "Others?"

"Yes, others," Nick said.

"I didn't know there were others."

"Of course there are. They are Indians. And this is what I wanted to talk to you about. I go to this place, it's called Braves' Point. These Indians lived here a long time ago, on this land, before white man, people like me, came here." Nick paused. "You following me so far?"

"Yes?" the puddle replied.

"And these Indians were killed; massacred; totally. Made extinct."

"All things die," the puddle said, a new confidence in the voice. "One tree falls, the other flourishes. Soon the one that flourishes will also fall."

"My, aren't we sounding intelligent today," Nick said.

"I remember things. The stars, the vast night sky. The turning of the earth itself."

"Wow . . . that's pretty heavy." Nick cleared his throat. "How could you know these things?"

"I was hoping *you* could tell me," the puddle said, sadly.

"We have to look at this scientifically. Obviously you were not *always* a puddle. You fell from the sky," Nick said, now circling. "So it would make sense that you remember things that you could have seen from the sky, like the stars, and the earth turning beneath you."

"Yes . . . that makes sense. And falling. I remember falling."

"Right. So, before you were falling, you must *not* have been falling."

"Correct."

"Which means you were in the sky," Nick said.

"Correct."

"You were rain."

"Yes, I must have been something before I was a puddle."

"Right. So we know that for sure."

"Yes."

They were at an impasse. After a silence, the puddle made a startling inquiry. "What were you before you were here, stranded on the surface of the earth, Nick?"

It was something Nick had never really considered before. Not only did the question make him stop and think, but he instantly had a new regard for his friend in the woods. No one he encountered these days wanted to talk much beyond the weather. Charles was always the one who asked him the difficult questions. Justine was certainly not high on life, and Doc Dugan seemed to be losing it—especially lately, he was "there" one minute and gone the next. His mother was basically a hermit, and Nick was unsure if it was her illness or the loss of her husband that caused her to shut down from the world. Who else was there? Blough? No way. Nutso? The Ghost? They couldn't even talk.

The mere fact that the puddle had breached the territory of unexplored thoughts made Nick feel closer to it.

"Before I was born? What was I? I don't know," Nick said.

"Well, then, you're as lost as I am, aren't you?"

Nick had to agree. Like the time after death, the time before life was a mystery to him. At the church he had gone to sometimes, they talked of heaven, but Nick couldn't buy it somehow—all those angels and marble hallways. No one had ever asked "Where were you *before* you were born?" This was a new concept, a new idea. And that was exciting.

"I guess we're both lost," he said to the puddle, and he leaned over, staring at his own reflection. The wind blew slightly, the water moved in tiny waves, causing his image to ripple.

"I'm starting to like you," Nick said.

"I like you, too," said the puddle.

Silent Prayer

"A what?" said Kemper, as he leaned forward in his chair and slung his elbows onto the desk top.

"A puddle," Nick answered, with a matter-of-fact look on his face.

"You're hearing a voice—in a puddle . . ."

"That's right."

Kemper stirred his coffee and scratched his head. "Another Indian . . ."

"No."

"No?"

"No. Definitely not an Indian."

"Nick, you know," Kemper said, rocking back in his chair, "you're supposed to be improving here . . ."

Nick said nothing. He blinked his eyes and cleared his throat, and readjusted himself in his chair.

"And what do you talk about with this puddle?"

"Well, a lot of things. Wars. Killing. Life, death. Um . . . oceans, huge cities, oil slicks, holes in the atmosphere—"

"Nick, just a minute. Hold it. You know, you're a very smart boy. Smart enough to have a little fun once in a while."

"I'm not making this up."

"Nick—please. Think about what you're saying. What if someone else told you they were hearing voices, in puddles, in the wind—what would you think? What if Justine told you she was hearing voices come out of the sink? What would you think?"

Nick's head fell. He had no answer.

"Think about it. See you in two weeks."

• • •

Usually he shook off his visits with Kemper but this one had bothered him. And usually he raced home, but this time he pedaled slowly all the way.

I wasn't lying, he thought. But Kemper thinks I was. Who cares what that nerd thinks, anyway? A few seconds passed, and then he thought, Maybe *I* do.

He sped up as he neared home. He saw his mailbox approaching quickly on his left and veered toward it. He held out his hand, got his balance, and when he reached it he opened the door with lightning speed.

But there wasn't any mail in the box, and he was so surprised that he almost tumbled off his bike. He circled back and looked again. The box was empty. "Hmm," he muttered, and looked at his watch. It was 2:00 P.M.

• • •

Justine sat at the kitchen table reading *Vogue* magazine, smoking a cigarette and picking through a box of chocolates. Nick went right to the newspaper on the counter, brought it to the table and sat down.

"Eating chocolates, Aunt Justine?"

"I know," she said. "It'll make me fat."

"Er . . . ," Nick added.

She dropped her magazine. "Nick!"

He raised his hands guiltlessly. "What? . . . I'm just tellin' ya . . ."

"Watch it, pal," she said, half-seriously.

"God, why does everybody hate me today?"

Justine picked up her magazine. "What do you mean?"

"Nothin'," he said, then spread the newspaper out on the table and flipped to the classified section.

Something caught his eye. He went over to the phone and punched some numbers.

"Hello," said a friendly voice.

"Hi. This is Nick Harper calling, and, ahh . . . you have in the paper here that your dog is missing?"

"Yes? . . ."

"Well, I've seen this dog, and—you have here black, short hair, shepherd-dobie mix . . ."

"Right . . ."

"Well, I've seen a dog like that."

"Where do you live?"

"Um, on Stanepote Road. Sharon Lake."

"Oh, no, son, we're in Bridge Falls."

"Oh," Nick said, "that's too far, huh."

"I think so, son."

"Well, you know a dog can travel . . ."

"This dog is pretty old, son."

"Oh, really?"

"Yes, he—"

Nick cut him off. "Oh, well this dog isn't old—the one I saw."

"Oh."

"No, he's about as strong as an ox," Nick said.

"Well, thanks for calling."

"All right."

" 'Bye-bye, now."

" 'Bye."

Disappointed, Nick hung up the phone, went back to the table and sat down.

"Did you get the mail, Nick?" Justine asked.

"Wasn't any . . . weird. Things are getting weird around here."

"Huh?" Justine said. She hadn't heard him.

"Never mind . . ."

He went upstairs to check on The Ghost.

He pulled up a few drops of liquid medicine into a dropper and walked to the bed.

The cat looked worse. Nick stopped for a minute and just watched it. Then he knelt, lowered his head for a moment and said a silent prayer.

When he ran his hand across The Ghost's back, it raised its head and looked at him, as though it didn't understand why it felt so bad. Nick had no answers. And when he slid his fingers underneath its belly, he could feel moisture with his fingers. The sheets were wet.

It had been urinating where it lay. Nick knew enough about animals to know that that was a very bad sign.

"We didn't even have time to hang out together,

Ghostie,'' he said, and then dropped the medicine into its mouth.

. . .

''How is he?'' Justine said as he came back into the kitchen.

He couldn't speak. He just shrugged.

Justine closed her magazine. ''Nick?''

He shook his head.

''You giving him his medicine?''

''Sure, yes,'' he managed to get out.

She noticed something was wrong. ''Takes awhile, Nick. Give it time to work.''

''Yeah,'' Nick said. His eyes met Justine's. He was crying. ''He's a good cat,'' he said.

She stood and went to him, and gently pulled his head against her and held him. ''Oh, Nickie . . .''

One

"DO you know anything about love?"

"Yes," the puddle said.

"Well, what is it? And why does it cause so much pain?"

"Love is, like the air . . . or time."

"Time?"

"Yes, it's there. But it's invisible. You can't touch it, or see it, but it is there."

"But why does it cause pain?"

"It doesn't. But misunderstanding it does. That misunderstanding is the cause of the pain."

"I don't get it."

"Love is something you do. Not something you receive."

The voice had a familiar twang; for a second it sounded like his father's.

Nick needed to hear it again. "Can you explain that to me?"

"Certainly," said the puddle. "Your father died. And you feel a loss."

"Yes."

"But it had to happen, his death. If not then, or now, then later, but it had to happen eventually."

"Yes."

"So it cannot be a 'bad' thing, his death."

"But I miss him."

"Love is not received."

"What do you mean?" Nick said. Now it *was* his father's voice. I'm imagining it, he thought. Everything.

"You cannot be loved," the puddle continued, "you can only love. Don't you see? There is a lot of sadness in this world because people expect to 'feel' loved. It is an impossible condition. Love goes one way. One way only. From your heart, outward."

Nick had no answer to that.

"Nick . . ."

"Yes?"

"Just because your father is dead does not mean you have to stop loving him. Do you understand?"

The voice. At last it sounded like his own.

Over the Falls

NICK explained to the squirrel that The Ghost was very sick, and told him about all the crazy things that had been going on. Nutso just looked up at him quizzically, his big black eyes void of understanding. At one point Nick tried to touch it and the squirrel backed off. For the first time Nick felt guilty about keeping it captive.

Later, he thought. I'll think about that later.

He strolled lazily down the gravel driveway to get the mail, kicking the stones around, struggling with his present problems. He hadn't been with his mother very much, nor had he visited Doc Dugan, and he hadn't reported to Blough's farm to dig the horseshoe pits, and the more he put these things off the more pressure he felt. And then Nutso—something had to be decided about him. The Ghost was wasting away up in his bedroom and really needed to go back to the vet. He missed—yearned for—

Pam Sue in a way that he did not fully understand. It all seemed too much. The only positive current in his life was his new friend in the woods. Only there, by the puddle's side, was he truly at peace. Even Braves' Point did not appeal to him so much anymore. The voices there were grating in comparison to the puddle, which seemed to be growing, maturing, becoming more intelligent with each passing day.

Again, there was no mail.

. . .

Justine couldn't believe what she was hearing. Anne Manning, a childhood friend, was on the phone. The two hadn't talked in years, not since they graduated from St. Monica's High School over twenty years ago.

Anne explained that Arthur Digny was her uncle. He had been stricken by a heart attack two days earlier, at the post office, as he sorted mail for his route. He died before the ambulance arrived.

Suddenly Justine realized why the mail hadn't come in a couple of days. She expressed her sympathy to Anne Manning, who had been assigned the harrowing task of calling the people on her uncle's mail route, and then, after discussing old times for a moment, and promising to get together soon, she hung up.

She was stunned. Justine, who had moved back to Sharon Lake after years of being gone, had gotten to know only a few folks, and the mailman Arthur Digny was one of them.

Arthur Digny. The godsend. A picture of goodness. Every week he would pile food and supplies into the back of his mail truck and bring the stuff out to Justine; he didn't have to do that, but he knew she didn't drive and she needed the help.

Justine liked his constant smiles and kind hellos. She envied him—he was one of those people who had come to peace with his lot in life, an achievement that seemed, to her, unattainable.

Breaking the news to Nick was going to be tough. When he came in, she hesitated. The last subject she wished to raise with him was death. She knew how fond he was of the man, how he ran up to greet him and get the mail. She knew that Arthur was one of the few people Nick had contact with in the course of a day. But she had no choice.

Here I am, doing it again, she thought. When does it stop?

Nick pulled a bunch of stuff out of the refrigerator and began making a sandwich at the counter, with his back to her.

"Nick—you've noticed that we haven't gotten any mail in the last few days . . ."

"Yeah, I know. Mr. Digny must be sick again or something . . ."

Justine moved over to him. "Not sick," she said, as she gently turned him to face her. "Mr. Digny—passed away, Nick. A couple of days ago."

Nick turned back to his sandwich. "How?"

Justine cleared her throat. "He just—fell over. At the post office, while he was sorting mail."

"I just saw him the other day. He looked good . . ." Nick said.

"He always looked good, that's for sure," Justine said, searching for a consoling ember of any kind.

Nick kept repeating, "Wow," and Justine had nothing further to add. She went into the living room.

Nick's appetite vanished. He wrapped the newly assembled sandwich in cellophane and placed it in the refrigerator. He settled for a glass of milk, then went out into the yard.

He sat for a long time, not overly sad. His thoughts hardly set on Arthur Digny; he wouldn't let them. Get back, he thought. Be gone. I've got a very sick cat and I have to get him to the hospital.

. . .

He rolled his bicycle toward town with The Ghost in the crate, and as he neared Main Street he decided to take a road he had never been on before. It led behind the stores, then down to the river and alongside it. He watched the water tumbling down a rocky cliffside into a pool of water at the bottom of a gorge. He looked at a small path that went off the road. It was just wide enough for the bike, surely he could navigate it, but he wouldn't try it with The Ghost there. Some other day, he thought, I'll take this Schwinn over the falls.

. . .

"Not looking much better, is he, Nick?"

"No," Nick answered as he watched the vet's skilled hands explore The Ghost.

It took the man some time to say what he had to say. "We're going to have to do some blood work on him, Nick. See if there's any—bad diseases happening . . ."

"Like what?" Nick asked, feeling suddenly weak.

"Oh, Fee-Luk—leukemia, that is. Or peritonitis, or

some kind of respiratory thing—there're a few it could be, just no way to tell, without blood work.''

Nick nodded, wanting to hear more.

''He hasn't responded to normal antibiotic treatment,'' the vet went on, ''so we have to start looking elsewhere for the problem. He's an older cat, a stray, we don't have any record of shots, none of that. He's feral, wild, those things can sometimes happen in these cases.''

Nick cut through the emotional shield the vet was trying to impose: ''Is he going to die?''

''Don't know, Nick. No way to tell. It's why I want to do a blood test. No sense even guessing until then. Okay?''

Nick agreed, giving up The Ghost's fate to a higher power.

''We'll have to sedate him to take the blood, so we'll want to keep him overnight.''

''Okay. Fine.''

They both stood with arms crossed, eyes on the cat. The visit was over, and Nick felt awkward about it; he'd never anticipated going home without The Ghost, and the image of it sitting in a steel cage all night unsettled him. But for The Ghost's sake, he remained brave; he stooped over, grabbed its neck, kissed its face repeatedly, and said everything would be all right. He left reluctantly.

He could have gone straight home but the empty cat basket afforded him some freedom. He zoomed Main Street, navigating the sidewalks and alleys, stopping to look into shop windows; he drank from the fountain in the park, and sat for a while in a wooden white gazebo, taking in the deep summer beauty of early August.

Then he saw it. Something—someone, moving across the long lawn. Coming toward him.

The blue-gray pants and short-sleeved shirt, and the over-the-shoulder sack gave him away; and the familiar gait, the limp-to-the-side hop . . .

" 'Afternoon, Nickie . . . ," the mailman said.

Nick closed his eyes and opened them again. Just to be sure. "Good afternoon, Mr. Digny."

The Great Dance

"THERE'S a movie in the video store, called *JFK*." Nick paused for questions. There were none. "I was reading the box. Here's this guy, a great President, I guess, and all that. And young, really young to be President. Anyway, here's a whole country, years after the guy's death, still angry about it. But it's okay. Somehow *that's* okay, but it's not okay for me to be the same way, and my father just died in January." He paused, his anger growing. "And it sucks. Everyone watches me—the doctors, Justine, they're watching me, I know it; they're checking me out, every word, every move. Is he sane? That's what they're thinking to themselves. I know it. So I have to act right. Be pleasant. Well-adjusted," he said with a sneer. "But what I'd really like is to just scream my head off. I'd like to ask them WHEN WAS THE LAST TIME YOUR FATHER'S HEAD WENT THROUGH A WINDSHIELD?"

He was too angry to cry.

"Nick, do you know that after life is life? That nothing ever really dies, it only changes form?"

"Yeah, sure. Shed your wisdom on me, O Great Puddle," Nick said and rolled over, facing the sky.

"I once saw a tidal wave, huge, splendid, omnipotent, and yet it fell and ceased to be, and became a thousand parts of a new image, which nature brought to bear."

Nick, irritated by the lofty nature of the remark, said, "Yeah, so what does that have to do with my father? Where is he?"

"He is here."

Nick shivered at the immediate and certain response. "Where?" He sat up, looking around.

"Here."

"Where?" Nick said, irritated.

"You. Like a wave, he hit the earth, and pieces of him spread out, and one of them is you."

Nick sat quietly for a long time, thinking about the statement. He looked around him. Something was different. Summer had passed a point, it was no longer at its mightiest. Here and there were signs of decay. Leaves were turning brown, no longer robust enough to handle the straight rays of the sun, curled at their edges. Bugs lay dead in pools. Then he saw it.

The puddle had originally crossed the path completely; now it would be easy to get by it. Nick felt a sadness swell up in him.

"You're getting smaller," he said to the puddle.

"Yes. I know."

"No . . ." It made him even more angry. "You're evaporating."

"Yes."

"You'll be gone, too . . . soon."

"Yes."

"Nothing lasts. Nothing," Nick said, depressed again.

"Nick, don't you know that you, also, will be gone someday, at least you as you know yourself to be?"

"Yes, I do. I know."

The puddle continued: "That is how it is. It is the nature of things. Do not fear death, it is not sad. Do the willows weep at the end of summer? Does a bird choose not to fly because it's worried about falling?"

"Oh, whatta *you* know . . ."

"I know a very clear sound; I hear it. And you can, too. The voice of—everything."

"Voice of everything, huh?" Nick said, a bit doubtful.

The puddle said nothing. For a long time. When it spoke again its voice came in a whisper. "Nick. I want to help you. Accept my help."

Intrigued, Nick rolled up his pant legs, took off his shoes and put his feet into the puddle. "All right. I accept. Go for it."

"All right."

"Let's start with a bang. Explain death to me."

"All right . . . Our elements are billions of years old. They are only in different forms. Constantly changing, from one form to the next. Moving, always. All things a part of all other things. Flourish and fall. Flourish and fall . . ."

Nick scratched his nose. "How do you know that for sure?"

"It is simply the lesson that nature has to teach you."

"And what's nature's lesson on happiness?"

"There are clues to happiness all around you. Nick?"

"Yes?"

"Is the world happy or sad?"

"Huh?"

"I want you to try something. I want you to look directly at me."

Nick obeyed. Leaning over, he saw himself in the puddle.

"Do you see your face?" the puddle asked.

"Yes."

"Yet you know it is not your face. Your face is not actually in the water, is it?"

"No."

"Then why do you see it there?"

"It's a reflection."

"Correct. Of what?"

"A reflection of—me?"

The image of Nick's father came up in his mind—Charles, in his long-john shirt and blue overalls, his hair drawn into a ponytail. His soft eyes. And soothing voice.

"Nick, it is a reflection of something that *is;* of everything that is, of everything that ever was. *You* are the universe, Nick. Being alive, being able to think, and speak, you are both interpreter and the face of the world. You can mourn forever, and the world will be a mournful place. You can live, remembering the dead, and the world will be a place that hangs its head in sadness. Cry. The world cries. Laugh, it laughs. Be tormented, and the world will be in torment. Think of gruesome things, and the world will be a gruesome place.

"Nature has a violent side, unfriendly to the fragile flesh of animals, but nature is no more violent than it is peaceful and comforting. The dying scream, their pain is real, but in death, they do not feel pain anymore. Nature is merciful, and neither you nor I know why, Nick. But we must trust it. Whatever the reason behind this whole thing we call existence, or reality, we can be sure of one thing. It's trying . . . it's trying for the best way. It's trying to happen the best way. It's all in how we see it."

Nick shook his head once. Still looking at his face in the water, he leaned down and looked into his own eyes. "Did you say that? Just now?"

"What?" the puddle asked.

"Just now. Were you talking? About nature, having mercy?"

"Yes."

"Oh," Nick said, "I was just thinking of my father, and I thought . . ."

"Thought what?"

"That it was his voice . . . that I was remembering something he said . . ."

"Nick, are you looking at your face?"

"Yes."

"Into your eyes?"

"Yes."

"Now, make an ugly face."

Nick twisted his mouth, contorting his muscles.

"You see? You have put a face on the universe, and it is ugly. It is not the fault of your atoms that you look so unhappy. It is your choice. Now, smile."

Nick twisted his lips, forming an ear-to-ear smile.

"You see? How beautiful you are? You do the sky and forest justice."

Nick closed his eyes.

And heard Charles speaking.

"I tell you, we humans are a complex permutation of universal matter. We separate ourselves from the graceful flow of things by our ability to think. I have watched wars, I have seen people kill, not out of any kind of natural mercy, but because someone wants this hill to sit on for a while, or that hill to build on. I have seen ships split apart, pouring oil into the graceful oceans, leaving dead fish in their wake. We may not only kill ourselves, but everything else.

"When nature kills something, it is merely time for that thing to die, its matter to return to the caldron for reassignment. When man kills, he destroys the grace of natural rhythm."

Nick's eyes opened as the voice changed again. "Because man can lift his feet, he thinks he is not a part of the earth. Though he breathes the air, he sets himself aside from the heavens, as a loner, living in and among things, but not as a part of them. Your father's death, Nick, is just another step in life's dance. Without it, the dance would not be complete. *Everything* is a part of the dance, Nick. Each rock, each molecule, each tree and person and ant—"

"And puddle," Nick said, breaking in.

"Yes. We are all one."

Nick lowered his hands into the water, and let it flow through his fingers. He thrust his arms in, noticing how the water hugged him, everywhere, almost became a part of him. "Water," Nick said. "What a wonderful thing."

"Thank you," said the puddle.

"Who are you?" Nick asked.

There was no reply.

And then there was silence for a time. Finally Nick said, "Do you remember the first thing you said to me? Remember? You said, 'Where am I?' Do you remember that?"

"Yes. And you heard a voice that was lost, that needed help. You see, listening is very important. Take the time to listen to puddles, and trees, and clouds. Then you will be a partner in the great dance. Right now you have one foot on the earth, where it should be, and the other dangles in the air, reluctant to participate, unwilling to let the dance be as beautiful as it can be. I'll tell you this. You will always get your best advice from puddles, or trees, or rocks, or clouds. They know their part in the grand scheme and are satisfied to let the natural rhythm of things occur."

"Well, then, who are these spirits at Braves' Point that haunt the land because they were so brutally killed? Who are these voices?"

"They are you."

"Me?" Nick said, incredulous. "Now you sound like Dr. Kemper. That's what *he* says!"

"Maybe he's right."

Nick felt anger swell up in him. He felt betrayed. He wanted to scream but couldn't even speak.

"Nick, those Indians, dead now for four hundred years, are not eternally in a state of being murdered, no more than your father is always dying, always in pain. The Erie Indians are four hundred years into the beautiful dance, Nick—the dance of everything! The great dance. They are now rocks, and flowers, and insects, or pieces of bridges, or even—even a *part of you, Nick.*"

Nick lay back on the ground and took a deep breath. Could it be?

"Nick . . . ," the puddle said gently.

"What?"

"Do you want to know what I was, before I was a puddle? I remember now."

"We already figured that out. You were rain."

"Yes, but rain is only rain for a brief time. While it falls. Before I was rain, I was something else."

"What?"

"A cloud."

Nick sat up. "Yes! Of course!"

"It is why I remembered the stars, and . . ."

"And trees, and oceans, and rivers. Things one could only see from above . . ."

"Freedom," said the puddle. "It is why I remember freedom. Roaming, sailing."

"What a nice thing to be. It really is too bad you're stuck here."

"Yes . . . I miss the sky."

"You were a cloud. That's beautiful."

"Yes."

"Maybe my father is a cloud, somewhere . . ."

"Maybe he is. You know, it's all right to miss him. But you must be able to let him go. Love him, with all your heart, until you leave this earth, but let *him* go, let him dance. And concentrate on your own steps, so that you do not break the beautiful rhythm of the universe."

• • •

NICK walked his bicycle through the rough wooded terrain until he reached the road. Then he rode to Doc Dugan's, but saw no sign of him. As he sat, arms resting on his handlebars, he looked at the Dugan farm. The house seemed ramshackle, unkempt. The lawn, which the Doc had always kept manicured, was grown so high that the pond was hardly visible. Nick felt sad. Though he felt guilty, he didn't want to see the Doc. Not now.

He went home, went up to his bed and fell into a heavy sleep, which lasted the entire evening and through the night. Justine didn't wake him.

In the morning he prepared for the trip he didn't want to make. He ate a light breakfast and rode his bike into town. He was shown into the vet's office immediately.

He sat in the room with his arms crossed.

The vet came in a few minutes later carrying The Ghost's chart. He looked at the papers, and then at Nick. "I'm afraid I have some bad news for you."

"What?"

"The Ghost has a disease, an incurable one."

"What is it?"

"Do you know what AIDS is?"

Nick felt his heart sink. "Yeah . . . sure . . ."

"Same disease, except it's a cat form of it. The immune system, which helps fight off germs, well, it's not working. Feline AIDS, it's sometimes called."

"For cats? Never heard of anything like *that* . . ."

"It's a recently isolated strain—it's relatively new to me, as a matter of fact."

Nick let it settle in. "So he's going to die?"

"Eventually it will take him. They can go up and down. But eventually, his immune system will give up, and he'll be defenseless against a swarm of other diseases."

The vet let silence happen. Nick swung his dangling legs in the air, and then asked, "What do I do?"

"Well, there are options. Some people might opt to put him to sleep . . ."

"You mean kill him?"

"Well, Nick . . . it's merciful, um—"

"I'm not going to kill him," Nick said resolutely.

"Well, if you decide to do it, it isn't murder. And when the time comes, it will be apparent. And I won't ever tell you to do it; you'll have to tell me. In the meantime, you can take him home. When he gets sick, you can give him antibiotics, which may or may not ease his suffering. He may even get better for a while. But Nick, it will not be pleasant, for you or The Ghost, I will promise you that."

"Could I see him, please?"

"Sure," the vet said. He opened the cubicle door and ordered an assistant to bring the cat in.

The assistant laid The Ghost's limp body on the steel table.

"I'm taking him home with me," Nick said. He picked up the cat and carried him out of the office. He passed by the secretary without a word, went out the door and right to his bicycle. As he laid The Ghost into the crate, he said, "No more steel cages for you, my friend. Let's get you into bed. *I'm* taking care of you now. And I always will."

Tip

JUSTINE watched Nick as he walked down the road with a shovel hiked onto his shoulder. He had said he was going to Farmer Blough's to dig some horseshoe pits. She had asked him no questions, just let him go.

• • •

Looking out, Nick couldn't see as much as a water tower. Not a house, a road, nothing. Nestled among three groves of trees he could see no one, and no one could see him on the obscure part of Blough's three hundred acres. Alone with the earth, he dug all day.

His shoes had cracked from jumping onto the shovel blade with such force, and both feet were now blistered, but he kept going anyway, as if purging something from his soul in sweat, ignoring the blood on the tool handle from his blistered, raw hands.

"It's—time," he said, slamming the shovel in. "It—is —time . . ."

Stretching his limits, he endured the pain. And by the end of the day, two square lots of horseshoe-pit size lay open in the Ohio sod.

• • •

While Nick was away that day, Justine sat with The Ghost. It lay, prostrate, in fever, mostly sleeping, oblivious. He should be put to sleep, she thought, but knew what that meant for Nick—the horrible trip down to the vet's, the death itself, coming home alone. Death. It follows the boy, she thought. It's not fair. It's just not fair.

When she heard him coming up the porch stairs, she went out to meet him. He was quite a sight. Completely filthy, bloody hands, his clothes tattered. At that moment, he seemed more a man than a boy.

"Nick! Jesus . . ." She went to touch him, but he warned her off with a slow and stubborn motion of his hands.

"Justine, please . . ." He held his palms out and walked past her and up the stairs.

He called me by my first name, she thought. That's a first.

"I need a bath," he said without turning around.

He knelt by his mother's side and held her hand. "Mother?"

"Yes, Nickie," she said, her glowing eyes resting on her son.

"This will be the last time that I hold your hand. This is the last time we will look into each other's eyes."

"Yes, Nickie," she said, understanding.

• • •

He soaked his banged-up body in the hot bathwater for a long time before he called for Justine. He could hear her clumping up the stairs and he called out to her. "Do you have your wine?"

"No," she said.

"Bring it. And two glasses."

• • •

Justine entered with the glasses. While she would very much like to have a drinking companion, she wasn't sure it was right to give wine to Nick. He was too young. Still, she sensed this was an unusual occasion, so she had poured him a little in a glass and topped it off with water. She handed it to him. He looked up at her from the soapy water and toasted in her direction. She lowered the toilet seat lid and sat down.

Nick began: "Would you tell me about my father when he was my age?"

A smile came to Justine's face. Nick could tell by her expression that her mind was traveling into the past. When she had called up the image of young Charles, she smiled and then her eyes let loose a steady stream of tears. Nick did not comfort her in his usual way. He watched her.

This is my time. Not hers. That's what Nick was thinking and she saw it in his stare. She grabbed a towel and wiped her face.

"He was—a beautiful boy . . . let's see. Well, when he was about ten or so, a little younger than you. I remember him then, a summer, your grandma and grampa and me and Charles, we went up to Vermilion, on the lake, to a cottage for a week . . . someone got him some Beatle wallpaper. Um, the Beatles, you know, the rock group, hundreds of little pictures of them, and he put it up on his bedroom wall. Very cool. Very cool. I don't know why I remember that so well, but that was Charlie, right there with the times. He had his hand on a pulse, as early as ten." She sipped her wine. "Hard to think of what a roll of that stuff would go for now . . ."

Nick swooshed the red liquid around in his glass and took a small sip.

"Do you like it?" Justine asked. Nick nodded. "Just drink it slowly." Justine went on. "He was very kind. Helped everyone, but wanted a lot of time alone, and when he was alone, he didn't like to be bothered. He read constantly. After a few years, when your grampa was dead . . . see grandma was pretty socially active, so Charles and I spent a lot of time together, well, not together as much as in the same house together. He read constantly and wasn't out screwing around very much; he was like a little man in a boy's body. In school, everyone looked up to him. He took school very seriously. It was like he was on a course; he knew it even at an early age. There wasn't anybody who didn't like him. It was like he had this great thing to do in life, and he was constantly preparing for it."

"What about all the stories about how wild he was? I heard a lot of people talk about crazy stuff he did . . . ?"

"Oh, yeah, when he got a little older he got a little crazy . . . but see, the world changed, and just like Charlie, he was right there at the starting line. He went hippie, before I did, and at first I didn't understand. Not just me, but everybody thought he had turned down a dark path, the wrong path. He would trip on acid up in his bedroom—''

''What? What do you mean?'' he asked.

''Well, acid—is a hallucinogenic. It causes hallucinations.''

''Hallucination? Right? I know what that is,'' he said confidently.

Justine wondered how he could possibly know. ''It's sort of funny, now, thinking back—'' She paused a moment. ''I remember, we were all having Thanksgiving dinner, and Charles came down and very plainly said that Jesus Christ was in his bedroom praying, and could we all be quiet until he was finished. I remember Mom folded up her napkin, dropped it in her dinner and ran into the kitchen crying. I had never done acid before, so I had no idea what was happening either, and Dad, well, he didn't know what to do.'' Her mind drifted off for a second. ''We were all worried about him for months, because these episodes would come and go, and otherwise he would be very normal, studying, reading, just like he always had. Later, it happened to me—like it happened to a whole generation . . . the drugs, the music, the ideas . . . then I understood what he was doing. He was on a search for his own identity, for who he was. He had to find it out for himself, and no one could go with him on the journey. It's something we have to do in life, discover ourselves, or rediscover ourselves, and not only once but whenever we're lost, when we lose our ground.'' She stopped and took another swallow of wine. ''It's hard to explain, that period, the sixties, and early seventies.''

''So then what happened?''

"The shooting. Kent. We were all in school there when it happened—Charles, Mary Lee, and me. That changed everything. We all realized that for all our talk of love and all that, there were still guys with guns out there ready to kill you—just for wanting peace in the world. It blew our minds. None of us were ever the same. Your dad, and your mom, and me, we were right in the middle of it all, and after the rifles stopped we walked toward this crying girl, and we saw a dead boy, and we clutched each other, and we cried, and everyone felt shame. The guardsmen, they were just kids like us, and they were as scared as we were, shaking in their helmets, and some of them were crying, too."

"Mom and Dad used to talk about that."

". . . and not long after that, your dad married your mother, and they moved back here to Sharon Lake and started farming the place. They were happy together, always. They lived here ten years before they had you. I moved to Kansas City with this guy and we lived together there for a long time . . ."

"What happened to him?" Nick asked.

"It didn't work out."

"Oh. Sorry."

"Well, you know, things happen. Things happen for the best." She took one of Nick's hands and looked at it. "You really messed yourself up, huh?"

"Yeah. I kind of went wild out there."

Justine sat back for a moment sipping her wine.

Nick waited a beat. "Justine, I want to tell you a few things." His legs moved in the water. "A very terrible thing happened to me when Dad died. You know that."

"Yes, Nickie. A terrible thing. It happened to us all."

"And I'm just now realizing that maybe I'm not so okay about it all, that something is really wrong with me." He watched her for agreement or denial. She gave no sign either way. He went on. "But some things are happening. I'm starting to see. You know, it's hard, from looking outside in, what one is. What one is like. How other people see you. Sometimes, when you look at me, I know you're worrying about me, wondering if I'm all right, you know, healthy, in the head. And Kemper. I know I'm there for a reason. Not every boy or girl goes to see a psychologist. Right?"

"Right . . . ," Justine said, nodding, wanting him to go on.

"And so I'm getting the idea . . ." He stopped, trying to figure how best to go on. "Let me tell you something that might scare you."

"All right," Justine said, shifting a bit.

"This morning, I saw Mr. Digny, with his mail sack, and he stopped and nodded at me, and smiled like he always did. And then he walked away."

It seemed like all the warmth had suddenly left the room. I shouldn't have given him the wine, Justine thought, it was a mistake. "Mr. Digny is dead, Nick. He's dead."

"I know that. But I saw him. Which means either there are ghosts walking the earth in Sharon Lake, or I'm insane. Right?"

Justine didn't answer. She wanted him to keep talking.

"There's more. There is a voice, which speaks to me in the woods. But I want you to know that this voice, whatever it is, is helping me get through this. I'm beginning to understand things, to be able to put them together, and I want you to trust me on this. I'm getting better. Mainly, I don't want you to worry about me. I'm going to be all right."

Justine half-nodded, feeling uncertain.

"Justine? Can I ask you something?"

"Sure . . ."

"Did you ever have hallucinations, on acid or anything?"

She nodded.

"Would you tell me what they were like?"

She was motionless, questioning the propriety of discussing the subject with a twelve-year-old. "Ah—you mean what were they like?"

"Yes."

"I only did it once. I was—um, in a bar, it had a pool table, and—" Her words sped up as she eased into the past. "The walls were orange, bright orange, and they were moving, curling, rolling. And I played pool, and the balls were—on my side, you might say. They'd—wink at me, like they were saying, 'Hit me! I'll go in!' And sure enough, they did. Then, later, I had to leave the bar 'cuz it got too heavy, and I went outside with my boyfriend and looked at the stars. They were melting, and dripping down the sky like wax, hitting the ground and exploding. Sounds pretty weird, huh, Nick?"

"It really looked like that?"

"Oh, yeah, and I think the lesson was, um—don't trust your perception of things; the mind is something that *perceives;* it is not reality itself. It's a viewer that you look through. And don't always believe what you see, how you see . . ."

"Or hear," Nick said.

This was like a conversation he might have had with Charles. He hadn't thought that possible. Maybe he'd never given Justine a chance.

"So, hallucinations can be good? They can teach you something, isn't that right, Justine?"

"I don't know . . . you don't *need* them."

"I'm scared," he said simply. He looked at her, right in the eyes. "Why am I seeing ghosts?"

She had no answer.

• • •

Later that night, Nick crept into her bedroom and woke her gently. Half-asleep, she said, "What, Nick? What's the matter?"

He whispered. "I need—to go away. For a couple of days. Justine, I won't be far away. Don't worry about me. Don't have the police looking for me or anything. I'll be fine."

Her mind was hazy from sleep. "What are you talking about?"

"I'm not well. Am I?"

"Nick," she said, and sat up.

"There are some things I have to face, and I have to do it alone. No Kemper. No Justine. Nobody. And I promise you that when I return, when I return . . ." He stopped.

"Go back to bed, Nickie, we'll talk more in the morning."

He said nothing. He stared at her.

"Okay, Nick?"

"You remind me of my dad," he said, and he smiled. "He had a really good sister, didn't he?"

"He did," she said, "and I had the best brother in the world." Her eyes began to fill up.

"I love you, Aunt Justine," he said, and let her head fall onto his chest, and lightly patted her on the back as her tears fell.

Barely awake, if awake at all, she lay back on the pillow. Nick watched her for a moment, then walked to the door. Before he left, he turned and said, "Don't worry. Don't look for me. I'll find myself."

• • •

He would be gone by sunrise.

The End of Summer

HE slept for only a few hours. When he woke up, it was still dark; he began packing his things. He put a sweater, extra socks and underwear in a large knapsack. In the kitchen he put together a survival kit of canned foods, nuts and chocolate bars. He packed two large bottles of Evian water and a canteen of tap water as well. He went out to the garage and got his father's collapsible fishing rod, a few hooks and slip-shot weights. He found a sleeping bag and attached it to his other gear. Lastly, he went into the kitchen again and wrote a very brief note to Justine.

Please milk the cows.

With that, he marched off into the woods.

His first stop was Braves' Point. "Hello," he said as he passed the burial mounds.

That was all it took. The voices came at him with full

force, and he instantly regretted having said anything. He tried to ignore them; he emptied out his shoes, attached a bottle of Evian to his belt with fishnet, did anything he could think of to block out their grating, complaining voices.

"Summer is falling, its majesty is not so great," one voice said. "Winter will come and destroy it. You'll see."

Nick had once been fond of the voices. They had been a source of comfort. Someone, at least, to talk to. But not anymore. They were too angry.

The puddle had warned, "They are you." If that was true, Nick didn't need to speak with them at all. But they persisted.

"We have missed you."

"We are the dead. The unjustly killed."

"Nick, Nick!" they called out, but he refused to answer. And then he realized that these spirits would be the hardest of all to kill.

Stashing everything under a fallen tree, he began his journey, which would take him deep into the woods, across the valley. It was a way of getting to the other side of town without going *through* town. He didn't want to run into anyone he knew. His only interest was getting to Pam Sue Healy's house.

Hours later, as he neared the Healy home, he stopped. And there he sat all day, watching the sky, getting up his courage, waiting until the sun went down before doing what he had to do.

When darkness finally fell, he built a small fire in the woods. He sat by it, saying over and over in his mind the words, *Pam Sue—I'm waiting for you. Pam Sue . . . Pam Sue . . .*

The fire crackled. Every sound was magnified. He could hear large animals rustling, probably deer, maybe fox.

Within an hour, he heard her footsteps.

Finally a figure of a girl stood, just yards from him. The moon gave just enough light to illuminate her features. It was Pam Sue.

"Nick? Nick Harper? Is that you out here in the woods? You scared me. I could see your fire from my bedroom window and I had to come out here and see who it was."

"How are you, Pam?" Nick said, his eyes downcast. She moved closer to him.

"Are *you* all right?" she asked.

"Yes, I think so. I think so. But maybe not," Nick said. "There are some things I need to say."

"Can I sit by your fire? It's a little cold."

"Sure. Sit down."

She did so, but not too close to him. He didn't want her that close.

Pam Sue looked back toward her house. "No one even knows I'm out here."

Nothing was said for a long time.

Nick couldn't get over how pretty she was, how ideal a girl she was for him. He regretted the times they could have had together, but never would. Had they both grown into adulthood, perhaps they would have married and had children. Now that would never happen. Nick was going to change things. He was going to put an end to their relationship once and for all.

"This cannot go on, Pam Sue."

"What?"

"You and I. I've got to get on with my life, and I've come here to tell you this. This is the time when I straighten everything out. I'm tired of all the things that confuse me, and one of them is you."

"How?"

"Tell me something, Pam Sue. *Tell* me something. Anything that I don't know.

"Like what?" She seemed confused.

"Like anything. Tell me how long it takes for a glacier to melt and cut a valley. Tell me how to iron a shirt properly. Tell me what the capital of Iowa is. Tell me something, anything, that I don't know."

He looked at her, but all he saw was her stare. She looked out, past Nick, into empty space, into nothingness. She had no response at all. "Pam? Can you hear me?"

"Yes," she said dreamily, detached.

Nick stood and gathered his things.

"Are you leaving?"

"No, you are," he said, and began to walk away. Then he turned around and looked at her one last time, lit only by the moon, her face an empty black space, her arms dangling at her sides, her clothes and hair blowing slightly from the wind. He turned away again and said, "Goodbye."

She didn't answer him.

She was gone.

• • •

He slept where he fell down, in a pasture at the edge of a woods, and woke up in the fresh morning, a bit disoriented, his face wet with dew. He drank some of the bottled water, then stumbled to the nearest small brook and washed his face and hands. It was time to return to the puddle.

When he got there, it had so diminished in size that Nick was startled. He stood for a full minute looking at the remaining few feet of water, the rest evaporated from the hot days or sucked underground.

"Hello," the puddle said.

"Hi." Nick sat down. "You are so small."

"Yes. My time here is almost done."

Indeed, it was a time of endings.

"What will I do when I need someone to talk to, when you're gone? Do you know how really alone I am here, out here, where I live?"

"Nick," the puddle interrupted him. "It is the end of summer. Soon it is the season of death, when things pass on, give in to what is nature. You cannot stop it. The grass around you that is so beautiful now will turn brown, and die. You have no power, Nick, over the life and death of things. Do you understand me?"

"Yes . . ." Nick said.

"So stop this. Let the living live. Let the dead die."

"Yes," Nick said, "you're right. I'm getting it. Slowly. Bear with me. I'm getting it." He stood up. "Okay, next, next place I have to go . . ." He collected a few things. "I'll be back." Once again he looked at the size of his shrinking friend. "So small. Your voice is not as loud. Remember, you were this big, stupid puddle of water."

"I remember . . ."

"I almost couldn't stand you."

"Yes, I remember."

Nick edged around a touchy subject. "Do you feel sorry? That we won't be able to do this anymore, I mean? To sit and talk about things, argue about things, just, you know, pass time?"

"Yes, Nick, I feel sorrow . . ."

"Sorrow. That's just a part of it all, too, isn't it?"

"Yes, it is. But it is only a reminder."

"A reminder of what?"

"That you *can* love."

Nick stood, nodding in agreement.

"Something you have . . ." Its voice trailed off.

"What's that?"

The puddle paused. Then, as it spoke again, there seemed to be a tremble to the voice. Nick was stunned. It was something he'd never heard, never expected. "You have—the gift," the puddle continued, "of love. Unlike the trees, and rivers, you have the ability to love."

"Yes . . ."

"You got it from your father."

"Yes—"

"And from your mother."

"Yes . . . ," Nick said, and quite unexpectedly broke into a fit of crying.

The puddle encouraged it. "You love your parents more than anything in the universe, don't you?"

"Yes," Nick said, gasping to hold down the sobs.

"And you miss them."

"Oh, God!" Nick screamed. "I miss them, I miss them so much, I miss them, I miss them . . ." And he kept repeating those words, and weeping, for a long time.

The Vigil

LATE in the evening Justine sat at the kitchen table across from the full plate of food she had set out for Nick. She looked out the window at the sun setting across the fields.

He had awakened her in the middle of the night. He'd said something but what was it? Don't worry about me? What had it been?

Too much wine. She had finished the rest of the bottle, something she had to stop. Her throbbing cranium and tight temples wouldn't let her forget that.

She stared at the note. "Please milk the cows." She knew what that meant. He had definitely gone somewhere. He would let a feeding slide once in a while, or a brushing, but never did he miss a milking. He knew it was bad for the cows and that was that.

But what was he doing?

Then it came back to her. In fractions. He had said:

Don't worry . . . and then she remembered—Charles. They had talked about Charles.

God, she missed him. Charlie. Big and wonderful brother. Watchdog. Reality Checkpoint Charlie. Grew the best indoor pot in the world. Had a secret touch with roses. Made food appear out of the ground.

Now she had his boy.

Then she remembered. She had cried and Nick had held her. And then he said, "Don't worry. Don't look for me." And that was it, that was all she could recall.

Fortunately, there wasn't a girl ever raised in Sharon Lake who didn't know how to milk a cow.

So Justine just sipped her coffee, looked out at the line of maple trees beyond the barn, and sent her love and best thoughts to Nick, wherever he was. He was definitely his father's son, but for the first time, she thought of him as her own.

Rising

HE didn't see the Doc in his usual spot by the pond. He went up to the house and tried the front door, but it was locked. Then he walked along the side of the house and looked in a window. He saw the Doc sitting in a rocking chair, not rocking—just sitting there. Nick tapped on the window. The Doc didn't respond, so he tapped harder. Still, his old friend didn't budge. Anxious now, he continued down the side of the house and to the back. He stood outside a screened porch. Some weathered aluminum lawn chairs were folded up and stacked against the back door. He moved them and the door fell open.

"Doc?"

Now the man was moving, rocking slightly, waving for Nick to come closer. As Nick crossed the room, he noticed how empty it was. There were just a few discarded crates stacked in the corner, and a vase, and an empty whiskey bottle. Nothing else, just those dusty old items. And Doc.

"You're going away," Nick stated.

The Doc nodded in a matter-of-fact way. "Movin' on."

"Looks a lot different, this house, with nothing in it," Nick said.

"Nickie . . . you're a good boy."

"I'm gonna miss you," Nick said.

The Doc smiled, and nodded. "You're a very good boy."

"It's not going to be the same around here without you, Doc."

"Movin' on," the Doc said.

And he stopped rocking forever.

• • •

Nick sat by the river until sunset. I'm not alone, he thought. Birds and fish are fine friends. And clouds, clouds that would someday fall and become puddles. They were good company, too.

That night he slept there, by the river. Toward morning he began to dream—about The Ghost, about Nutso, and, finally, about his mother. Only in the dream, while he could see both The Ghost and Nutso clearly, his mother seemed faint, indistinct. He could not see her face; only her essence.

When he awoke, he felt disoriented. Had he been gone two or three days? He wasn't sure. He hadn't touched any of his food. He hadn't even thought of food. He looked through his knapsack, but nothing appealed to him. He just wasn't hungry.

He did drink some water, but only because he knew he needed to.

He knew what his day was to be: walking, sitting, listening. Waiting for a noise.

For hours he heard only the locusts swarm, and the birds, and the rustling and cracking of trees, the wash of small rivers, even an airplane now and then.

But then, sometime in the afternoon, it came.

Blough's tractor. It appeared suddenly, rising off a hill, and it startled him. Nick noticed that the old farmer looked different. What was it? he wondered. Ah, yes, he was smiling.

Nick even had to say it. "You're smiling!"

"Nickie," Blough said as he nodded his head obligingly.

Nick made a motion. "Turn the engine off." The tractor chugged to a stop.

"Those were some mighty fine pits you dug, Nick . . ."

Nick put up his hand. "Please," he said, "don't mention it."

Nick walked around to the side of the tractor. "You know, Mr. Blough, this is some mighty fine country, this . . ."

"You betcha," Blough said.

"I picked that up from you, you know, mighty fine this, and mighty fine that . . ."

Blough just nodded, staring off.

Nick continued. "You never were a man to wear a smile, you know that?"

"Man smiles inside. Some men, I suppose."

"Yeah," Nick said, "but I have to tell you most people around here always thought you were sort of a, ah . . . an old grouch. Know what I mean?"

"Sure, I know what you mean," Blough said, smiling wryly. "Lotta real good whiskey do that to anybody, give 'em time," he added with slow country ease.

"Anyway, I just wanted to say, no matter what anybody ever said about you, that the words you said at my father's funeral, at the, you know, the cemetery; those were real nice things you said. Those people from Cleveland, you know, all his school buddies and stuff, they all said some nice things, and funny stuff, but there was something about Dad you said that really hit home. See, those other friends of his didn't know the part of him you did. They joked about politics, and, you know, college, and they remembered the kind of crazy guy I guess my dad used to be; but I knew him best, and I know what *really* turned my dad on the most. And you were the last to speak, and you said, "The man loved the land." *You* knew that about him. I knew it, too. And when you said it, I wanted to slap you five right there on the spot. You hit it right on the nose, Mr. Blough. My father loved the land."

He walked around to the front of the tractor and grabbed the crank. "I guess what I'm trying to say is . . . I know why my father liked you. And I didn't want anything bad to happen to you."

Nick spun the metal crank with a strong twist and the engine started right up.

"Good-bye, Farmer Blough."

Blough was still smiling as he rode off.

Nick closed his eyes, and listened to the sound of the tractor as it moved away, getting fainter and fainter. And when it was gone, it was gone forever.

Out of Darkness

HE still hadn't eaten, and though he hadn't begun a fast intentionally, he realized he was on one, and somehow the lack of food was making his mind more clear.

As another night fell, he made his way to Braves' Point.

He could hear the voices as he approached.

My God, he thought, they had never stopped.

They were going on and on about the same familiar things—their unjust deaths, cursing their murderers. Then they tried to entice Nick, tempting him with promises of unending friendship. He listened, but did not reply. He thought fondly of the spirits; they often had helped him pass the afternoons. They had helped him. But the puddle was right. The Indian voices were shallow in substance, their thoughts and observations were his own projections. And it never seemed more clear to him than it did now.

Eventually the voices fell silent. Now he would have time to think about the next morning.

It would be awful, he knew it.

Where would he find the courage to do what had to be done? The thought haunted him—he slept only for minutes at a stretch throughout the entire night. He was content, though, to have the minutes and hours to really think things out. To *decide*. He went back and forth in his mind. Should he really do it? *Could* he do it?

Early in the morning he made his decision. As the light appeared in the east, he stowed his sleeping bag under a fallen tree and then walked to the center of Braves' Point meadow.

"Good-bye, my friends."

There was no reply.

They were no more.

• • •

Now resolute, he moved quickly toward the farm. He ran down the long slope in the direction of the river, slowing to a trot only to catch his breath once in a while. When he reached the river he ran alongside it, following its curves near the banks and sometimes up and through the recesses of trees. But his pace fell to a walk when he reached the puddle.

There, he stopped. The puddle was so small now, just inches across. And when it spoke, its voice was so weak, as it had been at the very beginning. "Nick . . . please . . ."

Nick knelt next to it. "I can't stay. There's something very important that I have to do this morning, but I'll be back later today. Wait for me. There's still time."

"Yes, there's a little time . . ."

"Listen, just in case," he said, and looked into the sky.

The sun shone down on the shrinking pool of water; its heat was stealing his friend. "It's hot," he said, and swallowed. "And in case I *don't* get back in time, I want to thank you. You helped me get it together. I'll never forget you for it. I love you." He ran his hand across the surface of the water and then ran off toward home.

He got there by 7:00 A.M. Justine wouldn't be up for an hour. He absolutely did not want to see her, so he crept into the house, trying to make no noise.

The Ghost lay prostrate on the bed. It heard Nick, but hadn't the energy to lift its head and look at him. It looked so thin; once it had been a sturdy fourteen pounds. Now it was four and a half pounds of dying cat.

Nick wrapped him in a blanket and carried him downstairs. He fit him into the milk crate, got on the bike and rode carefully down the gravel driveway. He pulled out onto Stanepote Road and made a right, toward town. He looked back over his shoulder, feeling quite sure that Justine had never even stirred.

He pedaled as easily as he could, trying to make the ride as smooth as possible for The Ghost. The vet didn't open until eight, so he had time to kill. After a mile or so he stopped, where he had so many times, by the "Welcome to Sharon Lake" road sign. He took The Ghost out of the crate and sat on the ground, leaning against the signpost with the cat cradled in his arms. He talked to him, and stroked him, and let the morning sun shine on his face. For the last time.

Nick had decided that it also was the last time he would stop at this place. Or maybe he would stop here again someday, when all the pain was gone.

It was the very spot where his father had lost his life.

. . .

When the vet pulled his white Mercedes into his parking place he saw Nick sitting on the steps by the entrance. He knew it was going to be a bad day, because he knew why Nick was there, and situations like this one always drained him, made him want to go home, take the rest of the day off.

They hardly even spoke. Nick was fighting tears, trying to be brave. He knew that words might break him open. The vet didn't say much, letting Nick take the lead.

An assistant entered through the rear door of the examination room and placed some newspaper on the steel table. Nick laid down The Ghost, who by now seemed oblivious to all that was going on, and that was good.

The vet did some perfunctory things; he took the cat's temperature, looked him over. "He's really dehydrated. His liver is probably gone, swollen up. It's poisoning him. I could maybe put him on an IV, for now . . ." He paused. Nick said nothing. The vet continued. ". . . try and get some fluids in him, but I couldn't promise he'll make it through the day . . ."

Nick stopped him. "No. No more suffering. Let's just—" He couldn't say it. He tried again. "Let's . . ."

The words wouldn't come out.

The vet, knowing that it had to be Nick who made the call, went as far as he professionally could. "Do you want to put him to sleep?"

"Yes," Nick said, nodding, his eyes pooling up. He wiped the corner of his right eye and asked, "Will it hurt?"

"No, no . . . sometimes they don't go down easy,

though. If he jumps, it's only nerves, it's not the cat feeling pain, all right? Do you understand that?''

Nick nodded. Then he watched with horror as a large syringe appeared. The vet and the assistant quickly shaved one of the cat's rear legs.

Nick leaned over, and cupped The Ghost's head in his hands. He whispered, over and over, ''I love you, I love you,'' and looking sideways, saw the vet squeeze the milky fluid through the needle. The Ghost didn't move. The vet placed his hand on the cat's heart, for just a second. ''That's it,'' he said.

It was over. Nick, still holding The Ghost's head, looked at its empty eyes, its open mouth, its teeth, its frozen jaw.

''I'm sorry it had to end this way,'' the vet said, then he and the assistant left the room.

Nick was glad that they had left him alone. Still he held back his tears, but could not control his breathing. His chest shuddered as he inhaled and exhaled, but he did not cry.

''No more suffering, my little Ghost. No more.''

The vet, who had been listening outside the door, did not hear the usual crying. Thinking the boy had left, he pushed the door open. Nick was just standing there.

''We'll take over from here, Nick.''

''Yes, all right,'' Nick said. He was completely in their hands. They showed him out into the lobby.

''Sorry,'' the vet repeated.

Then Nick did something the vet didn't expect: he thrust his hand out and shook the vet's hand, then said, ''Thank you, Doctor. Thanks for everything.''

They walked together to the parking lot. The vet was truly touched by what Nick had said. Few people ever thought of his feelings. As Nick mounted his Schwinn, the vet said, "You had a tough thing to do, and you showed a lot of courage, Nick."

"Yeah," Nick said. He didn't really want to talk.

"And I know the time probably isn't right, just now, but there are plenty of little kittens who need homes."

Nick pushed off with his feet and turned a large circle. "Animals find me, Doc, I don't ever have to go looking for them."

He wheeled away, feeling terrible. Feeling wonderful. What he had to do now was not planned. He just knew what had to happen next.

. . .

Justine stood at the kitchen counter making coffee. Her back was to the door, and she was unaware that Nick was standing outside on the porch.

He watched her for a moment, truly happy that she was there. He still felt as though he were in shock; his emotions were moving in waves.

"Aunt Justine?" he said softly.

It startled her. She turned quickly and her hand flew up to her heart.

"Nick!" She gasped. "God, Nick . . ." And as she moved toward the door, he came in, and they embraced.

"Oh, Nickie, where have you been? I've been so worried about you, and then I got up this morning, and The Ghost was gone from your bed, so I was worried about him, too, and . . ."

Nick grabbed her firmly by her arms. "Justine, The Ghost is at peace. He's out of pain."

Her eyes widened as she realized what he was telling her. It hit her hard. "You mean he—"

"I took him to the vet this morning. He was put to sleep. His pain is over."

There was silence while she took it in. Then she began to cry, and he held her.

When she calmed down a bit he sat her down at the kitchen table and held her hand. "Are you all right?"

"Yes," she said. "Pretty silly, falling apart over a cat."

"No," he said gently, "not silly. It's better to feel sad than not to feel anything."

• • •

Nick was ready.

He started by asking her to go outside. She was pretty shaken, much more so than he thought she would be.

He sat her down on the top step of the porch and started pacing back and forth, trying to work up his nerve so he could say exactly what he needed to say. He waited a long time before he said anything.

Finally, he began. "Justine, look at me."

She did.

He sat next to her and took her hands in his. He felt his own tears coming.

She saw it happening, and began to speak, but he put his finger to his mouth, and shook his head "no"; she understood. He wanted to talk and did not want interruptions.

His chin fell, and he exhaled. He let his shoulders fall

and he relaxed completely. And let it happen. "My mommy . . ."

That's all he got out, and he burst into tears. He fell into Justine's arms. "She's dead and she's been dead, and I've tortured everyone by not letting her go."

Justine could not believe what she was hearing. She held him for minutes while he cried. "Yes, Nickie," she finally said, "she's dead."

"You've had to sit there and listen to me in her room, talking to her . . . it must have frightened you, so much, to think that I was crazy . . ." He couldn't get any more words out, he was crying so hard. She knew that what was happening was necessary, and she also knew it was important to push it even further.

She pulled Nick's head back, trying to hold back her own tears. She looked him directly in his eyes, daring him to brave it with her. "*When* did she die, Nick? *When?*"

Though he was heaving, he got the words out. "In—the —hospital. Three days. Three days later. The day—the day—"

"After your father's funeral."

"Yes. Then. She died then."

He tried to lower his head but she wouldn't let his eyes go. Her next words sounded almost angry, but she was intent on taking this to its necessary conclusion. "And who else? Who else is dead?"

Nick stopped sobbing. "Huh?" he said, slipping for just a second.

"C'mon, Nick!" she said, then almost screaming, "Who else is dead?!"

He just began to answer her. "Doc Dugan?"

Justine nodded, yes, that's right, yes, beckoning him.

"They found him in his folding chair, by the pond . . . a heart attack."

"When, Nickie? When?"

"Spring. May . . ."

"That's right. A long time ago. And who else, Nick? Who else is dead?"

"Farmer Blough?" he asked, for an instant unsure again, fantasy and reality warring for his mind.

"Yes," she said. "Say it, Nick."

The crying returned, and he spoke again through tears. "Farmer Blough is dead. His tractor turned over and killed him . . . a long time ago. When it was snowing."

"Yes, Nick. Keep going. Come on, Nickie. Come on!"

"Pam Sue . . . and her mother. Killed by the train. You showed me the paper." His voice trailed off, and then he was quiet.

Justine could hold herself in no more. Tears fell in streams down her face and she collapsed against Nick. They sat on the porch steps, rocking, held in each other's arms.

When the crying stopped, they stayed there, his head still on her chest, her arms around his back.

Then Justine uttered the three simple words she had never been able to say before. "I love you."

"I love you, too," Nick said, and he smiled.

They sat that way for a long time. Finally, Nick stood and stretched. "What a morning . . ."

They stayed for a while under the beautiful late summer

sky. Occasionally, Justine would start to cry again, and Nick waited it out with her. She needed some tissues, and headed into the house.

"I'll be right back, Nickie. Just—stay here, stay here, in the yard."

"I'll be right over there," he said, pointing toward the rooster pen.

• • •

He peeled back the chicken wire and whistled for his friend, the squirrel. "It's time, Nutso. It's time. Today, everyone gets out."

The squirrel noticed that its jail bars were down. Justine had come back outside, and as she walked toward Nick he put up his finger and she stopped. And she watched with him as the squirrel slowly, cautiously walked into the open yard and scampered off into the wild. Nick looked back at Justine, and as though their common genes fired simultaneously, they flashed a "thumbs up" at exactly the same moment.

• • •

"How about some food?"

"I'm fasting," Nick said in reply to her offer.

"Not while I'm around, you're not."

"Aunt Justine, I've got something very important to do," he said, looking up at the position and intensity of the sun. "There's one more thing, and I don't have much time." It would take an hour, he explained, and she agreed only if he agreed to take a sandwich with him and then take a bath as soon as he got home. While she slapped slices of ham on some bread, he sat in the yard, watching Nutso run here and there.

Justine returned with a small brown bag and made him take it. She embraced him once more.

And Nick went off to say his final good-bye.

Into Light

HE hadn't bathed in days, yet he felt somehow clean. Purified and still not hungry after four entire days. His mind was clear, his thoughts flowed smoothly and clearly as though across crystal, and he could control them—their weight, the amount of time they lasted. And he could judge his thoughts as well, like never before.

As he walked, he thought of The Ghost, and wondered where its soul was, but he knew as a result of everything that he had learned during this summer that the cat was fine, its pain was over, that it had gone back to "start." Still he could not fend off impulses that relayed his sense of loss; they flashed quickly through his consciousness, fleeting but real. Yet despite these familiar impulses, he was different. Something had been decided in his mind. Even tragedies have a good side, he thought. The Ghost, his father, Pam Sue, the Doc, even Blough—they were *not* gone. They, and all the dead, were not in a separate place; they were not lost or lonely souls. They were part of the natural cycle of existence. They were a part of a thing called nature, and *that* was deathless.

Yet Nick knew that the passing of the puddle would test him most of all.

He approached slowly, afraid he was too late. He couldn't make it out. His heart pounded and he walked a little faster. Then he saw it—a silver-dollar-sized spot of water.

"My God," he said as he drew closer and bent down onto one knee.

"Nick . . . Nick," the puddle said, its voice now almost inaudible.

"Hello, my old friend."

"Rising . . ." it said.

"What?" Nick asked. He could barely hear.

"Rising."

Nick had to bend all the way down, his face hovering just above the water. "Before you go, I have to thank you. Without you I wouldn't have made it. You have saved me from myself. Taught me . . ."

And then they came. Tears. The most yet. He sat back and cried. It was painful, but it was good at the same time. A relief.

"Nick!" said the puddle, mustering the loudest voice it could.

Nick, still crying, leaned forward to hear.

"Stand over me!" The voice now sounded desperate.

"What?" Nick asked, confused.

"Stand over me! Let your tears fall on me!"

Nick finally understood.

"Your tears will fill me," the puddle said, "make me—*larger . . .*"

Nick wiped his eyes, and moved into a position so that his tears would fall into the dirt beside the puddle. Then he sat up. "No," he said firmly.

"Fill me. We'll stay together . . ."

"No!" Nick said again. "Our time together is done."

"Please!"

"No! No, no, no! *You* taught me this . . . you're passing."

The puddle stopped pleading. "Yes. Passing . . . rising . . ."

Nick crouched so that his mouth was just above the surface of the water. "You don't want to ruin the dance, do you?"

"No," the puddle said, and there was silence for a moment. Then he heard the puddle laugh. "You've learned well."

Nick smiled. "And I'll be here with you, as you rise."

Suddenly he sensed something. Behind him. He could feel it. He could hear it breathing. And he could feel his own reaction, his muscles contracting into hard clumps, his heart pounding fiercely. Not now, he thought, not *now* . . . But it was too late. It was there.

The black dog was ten feet away.

Nick managed to stand up and turn around but then he was frozen in place.

The dog made a sound in its throat, an anxious, almost pleading sound. And then it sat.

That's unusual, Nick thought. It wasn't going to attack.

He got one knee free, and then the other, and moved backwards a few feet. The dog stood up.

He knew if he tried to run it would surely chase him down.

The dog eased toward him with its head turned sideways. Then it sat down again, keeping a space between them.

A waiting game, Nick thought. So he sat, too. They stared at each other for a long time. Then the dog began yipping and panting, his tongue going in and out of his mouth. He's hungry, Nick thought.

He looked down at the brown bag that he still clutched in his hand. He opened it, and took out the sandwich. The dog raised its head in interest, his ears alert.

Nick peeled a layer of ham off the heap of meat and dangled it in the air. "This what you want?"

The dog bobbed its head and yelped, all at the same time. Nick threw some shreds of ham and the dog caught them in midair.

"You know what?" Nick said. "It just so happens I was going to break my fast . . ." He ripped the sandwich into two halves, threw one to the dog and ate the other himself.

"No more," Nick said when the food was gone, holding up his hands as proof. "See? Gone." The dog lay down and turned its head, looking off into the forest. The ease of that action conveyed its trust, Nick realized, and Nick leaned back on his elbows, feeling the late summer sun on his face. What is more beautiful, he thought, the sky, or the trees and grass, or the dog maybe? It was a splendid-looking dog, with its shiny hair, its strong teeth, its eyes, alive and maybe even—lonely.

Then Nick watched as the dog got up.

What happened next seemed to take place in slow motion.

The dog went right to the small remnant of the puddle and sniffed it, but before Nick could move or even speak, it lapped up the water until it was gone.

"No!" Nick finally managed to get out.

But the dog didn't know, and it didn't care. It was thirsty. It looked back at Nick, quizzically, then sat down, and licked its chops a few times. Then it wagged its tail.

Nick realized his own mouth was hanging open and closed it. He leaned forward and saw for certain that the puddle was completely gone. "You drank my friend," he said, looking up at the dog.

But there was no anger in Nick's voice, and the dog knew it before Nick did.

It moved toward him, with its head turned a little bit, saying in its animal way that it meant no harm. Nick braced himself for another episode, but none came. His fear was gone. The dog sniffed him about the knees, and up his leg, and up his torso, and then it licked his hand. Nick slowly reached out and tapped the dog a few times on the top of its head. Within moments he was petting it, feeling its silky coat, scratching its skinny belly.

The wind picked up a little and began to rustle through the trees. A few leaves, already browned and dry, drifted to the ground. Nick lay back, exhausted, the black dog nestled against his leg; together they wandered off into sleep.

Above them, moving proudly and slowly in the sky, newly formed from the atoms of the universe, appeared a perfect cloud. In the soothing shifting of the breeze, a voice floated down.

"Good-bye, my friend," it said.

. . .

Nick did not hear the voice, however. He was through with hearing voices. But in his dreams he saw the cloud, and said to it, "We're free."